The Birds
and other stories

LONGMAN IMPRINT BOOKS

The Birds and other stories

Daphne du Maurier

selected and edited with an introduction by
Richard Adams
Head of the Sixth Form, Lord Williams's School, Thame

and a foreword by
Daphne du Maurier

with photographs by
Catherine Shakespeare Lane

Longman

LONGMAN GROUP LIMITED
Longman House
Burnt Mill, Harlow, Essex

This edition first published by Longman Group Ltd in association with Victor Gollancz Ltd 1980
ISBN 0 582 22290 7

Set in 10/11pt Baskerville 169

Printed in Hong Kong by
Sing Cheong Printing Co. Ltd.

Acknowledgements

The editor acknowledges with thanks the help and interest shown throughout the preparation of this book by Dame Daphne du Maurier, her agent Curtis Brown Ltd., and her publisher Gollancz; also the assistance of Robert Bristow.

We are grateful to the following for permission to reproduce photographs:
H and B Graeme, photograph of Daphne du Maurier; Gary Martin, cover photograph.

Contents

	page
Editor's Introduction	vi
Foreword by Daphne du Maurier	viii
The Birds	1
The Lordly Ones	35
The Pool	51
The Old Man	79
The Blue Lenses	91
Points for Discussion and Suggestions for Writing	125
Further Reading	132

Editor's Introduction

To her Cornish neighbours, she is simply Lady Browning, widow of a distinguished soldier and one-time member of the royal household. They will tell you that she is not a great one for local affairs or for serving on committees, preferring to lead a private life, seeing to her house, entertaining occasionally, swimming, walking in the countryside she loves. And working. For this unassuming figure, now in her early seventies, with the penetrating bright eyes and the frank warm smile is also Daphne du Maurier, one of the finest and certainly one of the most successful writers of our time.

She was born in 1907, the second of three daughters of the famous actor and theatrical manager Sir Gerald du Maurier and a grand-daughter of the Victorian artist and novelist George du Maurier. It is scarcely surprising that, coming from such a family, all three girls should, in the course of their lives, have shown strong artistic leanings. Angela, the eldest, has published several novels, while Jeanne, the youngest, is a painter who has exhibited her work both in London and in the west country. How Daphne came to be a writer she herself explains in the foreword which she has specially contributed to this book.

After being educated, like her sisters, at home, Daphne du Maurier was sent to a finishing school in Paris. She quickly formed an attachment for France and the French way of life and culture, and her parents saw that there was a very real danger at that stage of her settling abroad for good. It was as a counter-attraction for her that they purchased a holiday house on the estuary of the River Fowey in Cornwall. Their ruse worked. She conceived a love for her new home which has deepened with the years and Cornwall has become as closely associated with her writing as Dublin is with that of James Joyce or London with that of Dickens. Her first novel, *The Loving Spirit*, is the story of four generations of a Cornish boat-building family, while her fourth, *Jamaica Inn*, is a tale of smugglers and wreckers.

Her feeling for the west country was further strengthened in 1932 by her meeting with and subsequent marriage to the man who was later in life to become Lieutenant-General Sir Frederick Browning, for his attachment to the place was almost as passionate as hers. They spent their honeymoon on a boat he owned on the Helford River.

During the Second World War, while her husband was serving

in North Africa, Daphne du Maurier leased the Cornish manor house of Menabilly, which was to remain her home for over a quarter of a century. At least three of her novels were inspired by Menabilly – *Rebecca* (1939), *The King's General* (1945) and *My Cousin Rachel* (1951) – as were several of her short stories. In 1967, she published *Vanishing Cornwall*, a documentary study of the changing face of this wild but beautiful corner of the British Isles.

In 1969, after Sir Frederick's death, Daphne du Maurier moved from Menabilly to live by herself in a nearby house called Kilmarth, which she had used as the setting for another novel, *The House on the Strand*. Cornwall again appears in *Rule Britannia* (1972), but this time it is the Cornwall of the future. The book deals – like *Vanishing Cornwall* – with what might happen to the countryside and its people before the end of the present century.

As well as her Cornish books, Dame Daphne has written several novels and short stories with foreign – especially French – settings and has also produced some fine and sensitive biographies, notably of her father (*Gerald, A Portrait*), her family (*The Du Mauriers*), Branwell Brontë (*The Infernal World of Branwell Brontë*) and Anthony and Francis Bacon (*Golden Lads* and *The Winding Stair*.) She is also the author of three plays, while a number of her books and stories (including *The Birds*) have been turned into films for either cinema or television.

Daphne du Maurier

Foreword

Daphne du Maurier

The five short stories in this volume came about through observation, and I have found this to be a general rule, in my particular case, where short stories are concerned. Writing a novel is a different affair altogether though this may not be so with other authors.

I started writing short stories as a child, then as an adolescent, and was fortunate in having a maternal uncle who happened to be the Editor of *The Bystander*. He considered one or two of my short stories were good enough to be published, and printed them accordingly. He then advised me to acquire an agent – Curtis Brown Ltd – and they in turn found a market for the stories that were not suitable for *The Bystander*. So my career started. Anyone who is interested enough to follow this career through from babyhood to the publication of my first novel, *The Loving Spirit*, will find the full details in an autobiography now in paperback, *Myself When Young*.

Many novels followed *The Loving Spirit*, also marriage, and the raising of a family. What inspired these novels I cannot say. Some seed deep within myself grew, flourished, and finally found expression. Somehow, it resembled leading a double life. One half of me was devoted wife and mother; the other became in turn the various characters in the novel I would be writing, only to be discarded and forgotten once the novel was finished.

This double life I put down to being the daughter of an actor, my father Gerald du Maurier, who played so many different parts upon the stage. Therefore writing a novel, for me at any rate, was a form of acting.

It was only later, with several novels to my credit, or discredit, whichever the reader chooses, that I turned once again to short stories. Something glimpsed, something seen perhaps on holiday, abroad or at home in Cornwall, gave me an idea, and the story formed itself, but with my help.

The five stories which follow were all glimpsed from my home in Cornwall, or rather three of them were, if memory serves me right. *The Birds* came about through walking in the fields beyond Menabilly, where I was living at the time, and watching the gulls swarming above the farmer's head as he ploughed the soil. What if they swooped and attacked him? This was all. Then the story formed itself.

The Old Man had a similar source. There is a lake below the Menabilly wood at Pridmouth. I watched a male swan attack a younger swan, his own progeny. Then drive him away from the one-time nest towards the sea. The story formed.

The Pool was slightly more obscure. Two of my children were playing in the garden. My second daughter, Flavia, and my son Christian. I watched them play together, then wandered myself into the woods. I remember no more.

The Lordly Ones had its source in Devon, on Dartmoor, where I was staying with my sister Jeanne. One night I looked out of my window on to the village green and saw that a small group of moorland ponies had wandered down to the green under cover of darkness in search of food. The story formed.

The Blue Lenses. Here memory may be at fault. I believe that I went into a Nursing Home for a night to have a tooth drawn, with anaesthetic. The dentist thought it might be more restful to have this done in a Home than in his chair in the surgery. Most certainly I was not the unfortunate patient in *The Blue Lenses* but the idea for that particular story surely came to me then. The reader should realise that these five stories, with some others, were all written in what is termed early middle-age – my forties and fifties. It is true they possess a somewhat "other world" quality. Why this should be so I cannot say. I have never had any pyschic experience. The ideas, as I have said, came from observation, then were developed from within myself.

My early stories, written when I was a young woman in my twenties, and which I have been re-reading lately – having found them in a forgotten drawer in a desk – were very different. I seem to remember that they shocked my parents, not so much for their content but for a certain mockery of established things, and a premature knowledge of the ways of the world which I could not possibly have experienced for myself. Observation? Listening to the conversation of adults ignoring or unaware of my presence? I do not know. Nor can I say why I became a novelist, and a writer of short stories and a few biographies. A form of acting, yes. But also a need for exploration, not only of the world about me, but more important still, of the world within.

The Birds

The Birds

On December the third the wind changed overnight and it was winter. Until then the autumn had been mellow, soft. The leaves had lingered on the trees, golden red, and the hedgerows were still green. The earth was rich where the plough had turned it.

Nat Hocken, because of a war-time disability, had a pension and did not work full-time at the farm. He worked three days a week, and they gave him the lighter jobs: hedging, thatching, repairs to the farm buildings.

Although he was married, with children, his was a solitary disposition; he liked best to work alone. It pleased him when he was given a bank to build up, or a gate to mend at the far end of the peninsula, where the sea surrounded the farm land on either side. Then, at midday, he would pause and eat the pasty that his wife had baked for him, and sitting on the cliff's edge would watch the birds. Autumn was best for this, better than spring. In spring the birds flew inland, purposeful, intent; they knew where they were bound, the rhythm and ritual of their life brooked no delay. In autumn those that had not migrated overseas but remained to pass the winter were caught up in the same driving urge, but because migration was denied them followed a pattern of their own. Great flocks of them came to the peninsula, restless, uneasy, spending themselves in motion; now wheeling, circling in the sky, now settling to feed on the rich new-turned soil, but even when they fed it was as though they did so without hunger, without desire. Restlessness drove them to the skies again.

Black and white, jackdaw and gull, mingled in strange partnership, seeking some sort of liberation, never satisfied, never still. Flocks of starlings, rustling like silk, flew to fresh pasture, driven by the same necessity of movement, and the smaller birds, the finches and the larks, scattered from tree to hedge as if compelled.

Nat watched them, and he watched the sea-birds too. Down in the bay they waited for the tide. They had more patience. Oyster-catchers, redshank, sanderling, and curlew watched by the water's edge; as the slow sea sucked at the shore and then withdrew, leaving the strip of seaweed bare and the shingle churned, the sea-birds raced and ran upon the beaches. Then that same impulse to flight seized upon them too. Crying, whistling, calling, they skimmed the placid sea and left the shore. Make haste, make speed, hurry and begone; yet where, and to what purpose? The restless urge of autumn, unsatisfying, sad, had put a spell upon them and they must flock, and wheel, and cry; they must spill themselves of motion before winter came.

Perhaps, thought Nat, munching his pasty by the cliff's edge, a message comes to the birds in autumn, like a warning. Winter is coming. Many of them perish. And like people who, apprehensive of death before their time, drive themselves to work or folly, the birds do likewise.

The birds had been more restless than ever this fall of the year, the agitation more marked because the days were still. As the tractor traced its path up and down the western hills, the figure of the farmer silhouetted on the driving-seat, the whole machine and the man upon it would be lost momentarily in the great cloud of wheeling, crying birds. There were many more than usual, Nat was sure of this. Always, in autumn, they followed the plough, but not in great flocks like these, nor with such clamour.

Nat remarked upon it, when hedging was finished for the day. "Yes," said the farmer, "there are more birds about than usual; I've noticed it too. And daring, some of them, taking no notice of the tractor. One or two gulls came so close to my head this afternoon I thought they'd knock my cap off! As it was, I could scarcely see what I was doing, when they were overhead and I had the sun in my eyes. I have a notion the weather will change. It will be a hard winter. That's why the birds are restless."

Nat, tramping home across the fields and down the lane to his cottage, saw the birds still flocking over the western hills, in the last glow of the sun. No wind, and the grey sea calm and full. Campion in bloom yet in the hedges, and the air mild. The farmer was right, though, and it was that night the weather turned. Nat's bedroom faced east. He woke just after two and heard the wind in the chimney. Not the storm and bluster of a sou'westerly gale, bringing the rain, but east wind, cold and dry. It sounded hollow in the chimney, and a loose slate rattled on the roof. Nat listened, and he could hear the sea roaring in the bay. Even the air in the small bedroom had turned chill: a draught came under the skirting of the door, blowing upon the bed. Nat drew the blanket round him, leant closer to the back of his sleeping wife, and stayed wakeful, watchful, aware of misgiving without cause.

Then he heard the tapping on the window. There was no creeper on the cottage walls to break loose and scratch upon the pane. He listened, and the tapping continued until, irritated by the sound, Nat got out of bed and went to the window. He opened it, and as he did so something brushed his hand, jabbing at his knuckles, grazing the skin. Then he saw the flutter of the wings and it was gone, over the roof, behind the cottage.

It was a bird, what kind of bird he could not tell. The wind must have driven it to shelter on the sill.

He shut the window and went back to bed, but feeling his knuckles wet put his mouth to the scratch. The bird had drawn blood. Frightened, he supposed, and bewildered, the bird, seeking shelter, had stabbed at him in the darkness. Once more he settled himself to sleep.

Presently the tapping came again, this time more forceful, more insistent, and now his wife woke at the sound, and turning in the bed said to him, "See to the window, Nat, it's rattling."

"I've already seen to it," he told her, "there's some bird there, trying to get in. Can't you hear the wind? It's blowing from the east, driving the birds to shelter."

"Send them away," she said, "I can't sleep with that noise."

He went to the window for the second time, and now when he opened it there was not one bird upon the sill but half a dozen; they flew straight into his face, attacking him.

He shouted, striking out at them with his arms, scattering them; like the first one, they flew over the roof and disappeared. Quickly he let the window fall and latched it.

"Did you hear that?" he said. "They went for me. Tried to peck my eyes." He stood by the window, peering into the darkness, and could see nothing. His wife, heavy with sleep, murmured from the bed.

"I'm not making it up," he said, angry at her suggestion. "I tell you the birds were on the sill, trying to get into the room."

Suddenly a frightened cry came from the room across the passage where the children slept.

"It's Jill," said his wife, roused at the sound, sitting up in bed. "Go to her, see what's the matter."

Nat lit the candle, but when he opened the bedroom door to cross the passage the draught blew out the flame.

There came a second cry of terror, this time from both children, and stumbling into their room he felt the beating of wings about him in the darkness. The window was wide open. Through it came the birds, hitting first the ceiling and the walls, then swerving in mid-flight, turning to the children in their beds.

"It's all right, I'm here," shouted Nat, and the children flung themselves, screaming, upon him, while in the darkness the birds rose and dived and came for him again.

"What is it, Nat, what's happened?" his wife called from the further bedroom, and swiftly he pushed the children through the door to the passage and shut it upon them, so that he was alone now, in their bedroom, with the birds.

He seized a blanket from the nearest bed, and using it as a weapon flung it to right and left about him in the air. He felt the thud of bodies, heard the fluttering of wings, but they were not yet defeated, for again and again they returned to the assault, jabbing his hands, his head, the little stabbing beaks sharp as a pointed fork. The blanket became a weapon of defence; he wound it about his head, and then in greater darkness beat at the birds with his bare hands. He dared not stumble to the door and open it, lest in doing so the birds should follow him.

How long he fought with them in the darkness he could not tell, but at last the beating of the wings about him lessened and then withdrew, and through the density of the blanket he was aware of light. He waited, listened; there was no sound except the fretful crying of one of the children from the bedroom beyond. The fluttering, the whirring of the wings had ceased.

He took the blanket from his head and stared about him. The cold grey morning light exposed the room. Dawn, and the open window, had called the living birds; the dead lay on the floor. Nat gazed at the little corpses, shocked and horrified. They were all small birds, none of any size; there must have been fifty of them lying there upon the floor. There were robins, finches, sparrows, blue tits, larks and bramblings, birds that by nature's law kept to their own flock and their own territory, and now, joining one with another in their urge for battle, had destroyed themselves against the bedroom walls, or in the strife had been destroyed by him. Some had lost feathers in the fight, others had blood, his blood, upon their beaks.

Sickened, Nat went to the window and stared out across his patch of garden to the fields.

It was bitter cold, and the ground had all the hard black look of frost. Not white frost, to shine in the morning sun, but the black frost that the east wind brings. The sea, fiercer now with the turning tide, white-capped and steep, broke harshly in the bay. Of the birds there was no sign. Not a sparrow chattered in the hedge beyond the garden gate, no early missel-thrush or blackbird pecked on the grass for worms. There was no sound at all but the east wind and the sea.

Nat shut the window and the door of the small bedroom, and went back across the passage to his own. His wife sat up in bed, one child asleep beside her, the smaller in her arms, his face bandaged. The curtains were tightly drawn across the window, the candles lit. Her face looked garish in the yellow light. She shook her head for silence.

"He's sleeping now," she whispered, "but only just. Something must have cut him, there was blood at the corner of his eyes. Jill said it was the birds. She said she woke up, and the birds were in the room."

His wife looked up at Nat, searching his face for confirmation. She looked terrified, bewildered, and he did not want her to know that he was also shaken, dazed almost, by the events of the past few hours.

"There are birds in there," he said, "dead birds, nearly fifty of them. Robins, wrens, all the little birds from hereabouts. It's as though a madness seized them, with the east wind." He sat down on the bed beside his wife, and held her hand. "It's the weather," he said, "it must be that, it's the hard weather. They aren't the birds, maybe, from here around. They've been driven down, from up country."

"But Nat," whispered his wife, "it's only this night that the weather turned. There's been no snow to drive them. And they can't be hungry yet. There's food for them, out there, in the fields."

"It's the weather," repeated Nat. "I tell you, it's the weather."

His face too was drawn and tired, like hers. They stared at one another for a while without speaking.

"I'll go downstairs and make a cup of tea," he said.

The sight of the kitchen reassured him. The cups and saucers, neatly stacked upon the dresser, the table and chairs, his wife's roll of knitting on her basket chair, the children's toys in a corner cupboard.

He knelt down, raked out the old embers and relit the fire. The glowing sticks brought normality, the steaming kettle and the brown teapot comfort and security. He drank his tea, carried a cup up to his wife. Then he washed in the scullery, and, putting on his boots, opened the back door.

The sky was hard and leaden, and the brown hills that had gleamed in the sun the day before looked dark and bare. The east wind, like a razor, stripped the trees, and the leaves, crackling and dry, shivered and scattered with the wind's blast. Nat stubbed the earth with his boot. It was frozen hard. He had never known a change so swift and sudden. Black winter had descended in a single night.

The children were awake now. Jill was chattering upstairs and young Johnny crying once again. Nat heard his wife's voice, soothing, comforting. Presently they came down. He had breakfast ready for them, and the routine of the day began.

"Did you drive away the birds?" asked Jill, restored to calm because of the kitchen fire, because of day, because of breakfast.

"Yes, they've all gone now," said Nat. "It was the east wind brought them in. They were frightened and lost, they wanted shelter."

"They tried to peck us," said Jill. "They went for Johnny's eyes."

"Fright made them do that," said Nat. "They didn't know where they were, in the dark bedroom."

"I hope they won't come again," said Jill. "Perhaps if we put bread for them outside the window they will eat that and fly away."

She finished her breakfast and then went for her coat and hood, her school books and her satchel. Nat said nothing, but his wife looked at him across the table. A silent message passed between them.

"I'll walk with her to the bus," he said, "I don't go to the farm today."

And while the child was washing in the scullery he said to his wife. "Keep all the windows closed, and the doors too. Just to be on the safe side. I'll go to the farm. Find out if they heard anything in the night." Then he walked with his small daughter up the lane. She seemed to have forgotten her experience of the night before. She danced ahead of him, chasing the leaves, her face whipped with the cold and rosy under the pixie hood.

"Is it going to snow, Dad?" she said. "It's cold enough."

He glanced up at the bleak sky, felt the wind tear at his shoulders.

"No," he said, "it's not going to snow. This is a black winter, not a white one."

All the while he searched the hedgerows for the birds, glanced over the top of them to the fields beyond, looked to the small wood above the farm where the rooks and jackdaws gathered. He saw none.

The other children waited by the bus-stop, muffled, hooded like Jill, the faces white and pinched with cold.

Jill ran to them, waving. "My Dad says it won't snow," she called, "it's going to be a black winter."

She said nothing of the birds. She began to push and struggle with another little girl. The bus came ambling up the hill. Nat saw her on to it, then turned and walked back towards the farm. It was not his day for work, but he wanted to satisfy himself that all was well. Jim, the cowman, was clattering in the yard.

"Boss around?" asked Nat.

"Gone to market," said Jim. "It's Tuesday, isn't it?"

He clumped off round the corner of a shed. He had no time for Nat. Nat was said to be superior. Read books, and the like. Nat had forgotten it was Tuesday. This showed how the events of the preceding night had shaken him. He went to the back door of the farm-house and heard Mrs Trigg singing in the kitchen, the wireless making a background to her song.

"Are you there, missus?" called out Nat.

She came to the door, beaming, broad, a good-tempered woman.

"Hullo, Mr Hocken," she said. "Can you tell me where this cold is coming from? Is it Russia? I've never seen such a change. And it's going on, the wireless says. Something to do with the Arctic circle."

"We didn't turn on the wireless this morning," said Nat. "Fact is, we had trouble in the night."

"Kiddies poorly?"

"No . . ." He hardly knew how to explain it. Now, in daylight, the battle of the birds would sound absurd.

He tried to tell Mrs Trigg what had happened, but he could see from her eyes that she thought his story was the result of a nightmare.

"Sure they were real birds," she said, smiling, "with proper feathers and all? Not the funny-shaped kind, that the men see after closing hours on a Saturday night?"

"Mrs Trigg," he said, "there are fifty dead birds, robins, wrens, and such, lying low on the floor of the children's bedroom. They went for me; they tried to go for young Johnny's eyes."

Mrs Trigg stared at him doubtfully.

"Well there, now," she answered, "I suppose the weather brought them. Once in the bedroom, they wouldn't know where they were to. Foreign birds maybe, from that Arctic circle."

"No," said Nat, "they were the birds you see about here every day."

"Funny thing," said Mrs Trigg, "no explaining it, really. You ought to write up and ask the *Guardian*. They'd have some answer for it. Well, I must be getting on."

She nodded, smiled, and went back into the kitchen.

Nat, dissatisfied, turned to the farm-gate. Had it not been for those corpses on the bedroom floor, which he must now collect and bury somewhere, he would have considered the tale exaggeration too.

Jim was standing by the gate.

"Had any trouble with the birds?" asked Nat.

"Birds? What birds?"

"We got them up our place last night. Scores of them, came in the children's bedroom. Quite savage they were."

"Oh?" It took time for anything to penetrate Jim's head. "Never heard of birds acting savage," he said at length. "They get tame, like, sometimes. I've seen them come to the windows for crumbs."

"These birds last night weren't tame."

"No? Cold maybe. Hungry. You put out some crumbs."

Jim was no more interested than Mrs Trigg had been. It was, Nat thought, like air-raids in the war. No one down this end of the country knew what the Plymouth folk had seen and suffered. You had to endure something yourself before it touched you. He walked back along the lane and crossed the stile to his cottage. He found his wife in the kitchen with young Johnny.

"See anyone?" she asked.

"Mrs Trigg and Jim," he answered. "I don't think they believed me. Anyway, nothing wrong up there."

"You might take the birds away," she said. "I daren't go into the room to make the beds until you do. I'm scared."

"Nothing to scare you now," said Nat. "They're dead, aren't they?"

He went up with a sack and dropped the stiff bodies into it, one by one. Yes, there were fifty of them, all told. Just the ordinary common birds of the hedgerow, nothing as large even as a thrush.

It must have been fright that made them act the way they did. Blue tits, wrens, it was incredible to think of the power of their small beaks, jabbing at his face and hands the night before. He took the sack out into the garden and was faced now with a fresh problem. The ground was too hard to dig. It was frozen solid, yet no snow had fallen, nothing had happened in the past hours but the coming of the east wind. It was unnatural, queer. The weather prophets must be right. The change was something connected with the Arctic circle.

The wind seemed to cut him to the bone as he stood there, uncertainly, holding the sack. He could see the white-capped seas breaking down under in the bay. He decided to take the birds to the shore and bury them.

When he reached the beach below the headland he could scarcely stand, the force of the east wind was so strong. It hurt to draw breath, and his bare hands were blue. Never had he known such cold, not in all the bad winters he could remember. It was low tide. He crunched his way over the shingle to the softer sand and then, his back to the wind, ground a pit in the sand with his heel. He meant to drop the birds into it, but as he opened up the sack the force of the wind carried them, lifted them, as though in flight again, and they were blown away from him along the beach, tossed like feathers, spread and scattered, the bodies of the fifty frozen birds. There was something ugly in the sight. He did not like it. The dead birds were swept away from him by the wind.

"The tide will take them when it turns," he said to himself.

He looked out to sea and watched the crested breakers, combing green. They rose stiffly, curled, and broke again, and because it was ebb tide the roar was distant, more remote, lacking the sound and thunder of the flood.

Then he saw them. The gulls. Out there, riding the seas.

What he had thought at first to be the white caps of the waves were gulls. Hundreds, thousands, tens of thousands . . . They rose and fell in the trough of the seas, heads to the wind, like a mighty fleet at anchor, waiting on the tide. To eastward, and to the west, the gulls were there. They stretched as far as his eye could reach, in close formation, line upon line. Had the sea been still they would have covered the bay like a white cloud, head to head, body packed to body. Only the east wind, whipping the sea to breakers, hid them from the shore.

Nat turned, and leaving the beach climbed the steep path home. Someone should know of this. Someone should be told.

Something was happening, because of the east wind and the weather, that he did not understand. He wondered if he should go to the call-box by the bus-stop and ring up the police. Yet what could they do? What could anyone do? Tens and thousands of gulls riding the sea there, in the bay, because of storm, because of hunger. The police would think him mad, or drunk, or take the statement from him with great calm. "Thank you. Yes, the matter has already been reported. The hard weather is driving the birds inland in great numbers." Nat looked about him. Still no sign of any other bird. Perhaps the cold had sent them all from up country? As he drew near to the cottage his wife came to meet him, at the door. She called to him, excited. "Nat," she said, "it's on the wireless. They've just read out a special news bulletin. I've written it down."

"What's on the wireless?" he said.

"About the birds," she said. "It's not only here, it's everywhere. In London, all over the country. Something has happened to the birds."

Together they went into the kitchen. He read the piece of paper lying on the table.

"Statement from the Home Office at eleven a.m. today. Reports from all over the country are coming in hourly about the vast quantity of birds flocking above towns, villages, and outlying districts, causing obstruction and damage and even attacking individuals. It is thought that the Arctic air stream, at present covering the British Isles, is causing birds to migrate south in immense numbers, and that intense hunger may drive these birds to attack human beings. Householders are warned to see to their windows, doors, and chimneys, and to take reasonable precautions for the safety of their children. A further statement will be issued later."

A kind of excitement seized Nat; he looked at his wife in triumph.

"There you are," he said, "let's hope they'll hear that at the farm. Mrs Trigg will know it wasn't any story. It's true. All over the country. I've been telling myself all morning there's something wrong. And just now, down on the beach, I looked out to sea and there are gulls, thousands of them, tens of thousands, you couldn't put a pin between their heads, and they're all out there, riding on the sea, waiting."

"What are they waiting for, Nat?" she asked.

He stared at her, then looked down again at the piece of paper.

"I don't know," he said slowly. "It says here the birds are hungry."

He went over to the drawer where he kept his hammer and tools.

"What are you going to do, Nat?"

"See to the windows and the chimneys too, like they tell you."

"You think they would break in, with the windows shut? Those sparrows and robins and such? Why, how could they?"

He did not answer. He was not thinking of the robins and the sparrows. He was thinking of the gulls. . . .

He went upstairs and worked there the rest of the morning, boarding the windows of the bedrooms, filling up the chimney bases. Good job it was his free day and he was not working at the farm. It reminded him of the old days, at the beginning of the war. He was not married then, and he had made all the blackout boards for his mother's house in Plymouth. Made the shelter too. Not that it had been of any use, when the moment came. He wondered if they would take these precautions up at the farm. He doubted it. Too easy-going, Harry Trigg and his missus. Maybe they'd laugh at the whole thing. Go off to a dance or a whist drive.

"Dinner's ready." She called him, from the kitchen.

"All right. Coming down."

He was pleased with his handiwork. The frames fitted nicely over the little panes and at the base of the chimneys.

When dinner was over and his wife was washing up, Nat switched on the one o'clock news. The same announcement was repeated, the one which she had taken down during the morning, but the news bulletin enlarged upon it. "The flocks of birds have caused dislocation in all areas," read the announcer, "and in London the sky was so dense at ten o'clock this morning that it seemed as if the city was covered by a vast black cloud.

"The birds settled on roof-tops, on window ledges and on chimneys. The species included blackbird, thrush, the common house-sparrow, and, as might be expected in the metropolis, a vast quantity of pigeons and starlings, and that frequenter of the London river, the black-headed gull. The sight has been so unusual that traffic came to a standstill in many thoroughfares, work was abandoned in shops and offices, and the streets and pavements were crowded with people standing about to watch the birds."

Various incidents were recounted, the suspected reason of cold and hunger stated again, and warnings to householders repeated.

The announcer's voice was smooth and suave. Nat had the impression that this man, in particular, treated the whole business as he would an elaborate joke. There would be others like him, hundreds of them, who did not know what it was to struggle in darkness with a flock of birds. There would be parties tonight in London, like the ones they gave on election nights. People standing about, shouting and laughing, getting drunk. "Come and watch the birds!"

Nat switched off the wireless. He got up and started work on the kitchen windows. His wife watched him, young Johnny at her heels.

"What, boards for down here too?" she said. "Why, I'll have to light up before three o'clock. I see no call for boards down here."

"Better be sure than sorry," answered Nat. "I'm not going to take any chances."

"What they ought to do," she said, "is to call the army out and shoot the birds. That would soon scare them off."

"Let them try," said Nat. "How'd they set about it?"

"They have the army to the docks," she answered, "when the dockers strike. The soldiers go down and unload the ships."

"Yes," said Nat, "and the population of London is eight million or more. Think of all the buildings, and the flats, and houses. Do you think they've enough soldiers to go round shooting birds from every roof?"

"I don't know. But something should be done. They ought to do something."

Nat thought to himself that "they" were no doubt considering the problem at that very moment, but whatever "they" decided to do in London and the big cities would not help the people here, three hundred miles away. Each householder must look after his own.

"How are we off for food?" he said.

"Now, Nat, whatever next?"

"Never mind. What have you got in the larder?"

"It's shopping day tomorrow, you know that. I don't keep uncooked food hanging about, it goes off. Butcher doesn't call till the day after. But I can bring back something when I go in tomorrow."

Nat did not want to scare her. He thought it possible that she might not go to town tomorrow. He looked in the larder for himself, and in the cupboard where she kept her tins. They would do, for a couple of days. Bread was low.

"What about the baker?"

"He comes tomorrow too."

He saw she had flour. If the baker did not call she had enough to bake one loaf.

"We'd be better off in the old days," he said, "when the women baked twice a week, and had pilchards salted, and there was food for a family to last a siege, if need be."

"I've tried the children with tinned fish, they don't like it," she said.

Nat went on hammering the boards across the kitchen windows. Candles. They were low in candles too. That must be another thing she meant to buy tomorrow. Well, it could not be helped. They must go early to bed tonight. That was, if . . .

He got up and went out of the back door and stood in the garden, looking down towards the sea. There had been no sun all day, and now, at barely three o'clock, a kind of darkness had already come, the sky sullen, heavy, colourless like salt. He could hear the vicious sea drumming on the rocks. He walked down the path, half-way to the beach. And then he stopped. He could see the tide had turned. The rock that had shown in mid-morning was now covered, but it was not the sea that held his eyes. The gulls had risen. They were circling, hundreds of them, thousands of them, lifting their wings against the wind. It was the gulls that made the darkening of the sky. And they were silent. They made not a sound. They just went on soaring and circling, rising, falling, trying their strength against the wind.

Nat turned. He ran up the path, back to the cottage.

"I'm going for Jill," he said. "I'll wait for her, at the bus-stop."

"What's the matter?" asked his wife. "You've gone quite white."

"Keep Johnny inside," he said. " Keep the door shut. Light up now, and draw the curtains."

"It's only just gone three," she said.

"Never mind. Do what I tell you."

He looked inside the toolshed, outside the back door. Nothing there of much use. A spade was too heavy, and a fork no good. He took the hoe. It was the only possible tool, and light enough to carry.

He started walking up the lane to the bus-stop, and now and again glanced back over his shoulder.

The gulls had risen higher now, their circles were broader, wider, they were spreading out in huge formation across the sky.

He hurried on; although he knew the bus would not come to the top of the hill before four o'clock he had to hurry. He passed no one on the way. He was glad of this. No time to stop and chatter.

At the top of the hill he waited. He was much too soon. There was half an hour still to go. The east wind came whipping across the fields from the higher ground. He stamped his feet and blew upon his hands. In the distance he could see the clay hills, white and clean, against the heavy pallor of the sky. Something black rose from behind them, like a smudge at first, then widening, becoming deeper, and the smudge became a cloud, and the cloud divided again into five other clouds, spreading north, east, south and west, and they were not clouds at all; they were birds. He watched them travel across the sky, and as one section passed overhead, within two or three hundred feet of him, he knew, from their speed, they were bound inland, up country, they had no business with the people here on the peninsula. They were rooks, crows, jackdaws, magpies, jays, all birds that usually preyed upon the smaller species; but this afternoon they were bound on some other mission.

"They've been given the towns," thought Nat, "they know what they have to do. We don't matter so much here. The gulls will serve for us. The others go to the towns."

He went to the call-box, stepped inside and lifted the receiver. The exchange would do. They would pass the message on.

"I'm speaking from Highway," he said, "by the bus-stop. I want to report large formations of birds travelling up country. The gulls are also forming in the bay."

"All right," answered the voice, laconic, weary.

"You'll be sure and pass this message on to the proper quarter?"

"Yes . . . yes . . .' Impatient now, fed-up. The buzzing note resumed.

"She's another," thought Nat, "she doesn't care. Maybe she's had to answer calls all day. She hopes to go to the pictures tonight. She'll squeeze some fellow's hand, and point up at the sky, and 'Look at all them birds!' She doesn't care."

The bus came lumbering up the hill. Jill climbed out and three or four other children. The bus went on towards the town.

"What's the hoe for, Dad?"

They crowded around him, laughing, pointing.

"I just brought it along," he said. "Come on now, let's get

home. It's cold, no hanging about. Here, you. I'll watch you across the fields, see how fast you can run."

He was speaking to Jill's companions who came from different families, living in the council houses. A short cut would take them to the cottages.

"We want to play a bit in the lane," said one of them.

"No, you don't. You go off home, or I'll tell your mammy."

They whispered to one another, round-eyed, then scuttled off across the fields. Jill stared at her father, her mouth sullen.

"We always play in the lane," she said.

"Not tonight, you don't," he said. "Come on now, no dawdling."

He could see the gulls now, circling the fields, coming in towards the land. Still silent. Still no sound.

"Look, Dad, look over there, look at all the gulls."

"Yes. Hurry, now."

"Where are they flying to? Where are they going?"

"Up country, I dare say. Where it's warmer."

He seized her hand and dragged her after him along the lane.

"Don't go so fast. I can't keep up."

The gulls were copying the rooks and crows. They were spreading out in formation across the sky. They headed, in bands of thousands, to the four compass points.

"Dad, what is it? What are the gulls doing?"

They were not intent upon their flight, as the crows, as the jackdaws had been. They still circled overhead. Nor did they fly so high. It was as though they waited upon some signal. As though some decision had yet to be given. The order was not clear.

"Do you want me to carry you, Jill? Here, come pick-a-back."

This way he might put on speed; but he was wrong. Jill was heavy. She kept slipping. And she was crying too. His sense of urgency, of fear, had communicated itself to the child.

"I wish the gulls would go away. I don't like them. They're coming closer to the lane."

He put her down again. He started running, swinging Jill after him. As they went past the farm turning he saw the farmer backing his car out of the garage. Nat called to him.

"Can you give us a lift?" he said.

"What's that?"

Mr Trigg turned in the driving seat and stared at them. Then a smile came to his cheerful, rubicund face.

"It looks as though we're in for some fun," he said. "Have

you seen the gulls? Jim and I are going to take a crack at them. Everyone's gone bird crazy, talking of nothing else. I hear you were troubled in the night. Want a gun?"

Nat shook his head.

The small car was packed. There was just room for Jill, if she crouched on top of petrol tins on the back seat.

"I don't want a gun," said Nat, "but I'd be obliged if you'd run Jill home. She's scared of the birds."

He spoke briefly. He did not want to talk in front of Jill.

"O.K.," said the farmer, "I'll take her home. Why don't you stop behind and join the shooting match? We'll make the feathers fly."

Jill climbed in, and turning the car the driver sped up the lane. Nat followed after. Trigg must be crazy. What use was a gun against a sky of birds?

Now Nat was not responsible for Jill he had time to look about him. The birds were circling still, above the fields. Mostly herring gull, but the black-backed gull amongst them. Usually they kept apart. Now they were united. Some bond had brought them together. It was the black-backed gull that attacked the smaller birds, and even new-born lambs, so he'd heard. He'd never seen it done. He remembered this now, though, looking above him in the sky. They were coming in towards the farm. They were circling lower in the sky, and the black-backed gulls were to the front, the black-backed gulls were leading. The farm, then, was their target. They were making for the farm.

Nat increased his pace towards his own cottage. He saw the farmer's car turn and come back along the lane. It drew up beside him with a jerk.

"The kid has run inside," said the farmer. "Your wife was watching for her. Well, what do you make of it? They're saying in town the Russians have done it. The Russians have poisoned the birds."

"How could they do that?" asked Nat.

"Don't ask me. You know how stories get around. Will you join my shooting match?"

"No, I'll get along home. The wife will be worried else."

"My missus says if you could eat gull, there'd be some sense in it," said Trigg, "we'd have roast gull, baked gull, and pickle 'em into the bargain. You wait until I let off a few barrels into the brutes. That'll scare 'em."

"Have you boarded your windows?" asked Nat.

"No. Lot of nonsense. They like to scare you on the wireless. I've had more to do today than to go round boarding up my windows."

"I'd board them now, if I were you."

"Garn. You're windy. Like to come to our place to sleep?"

"No, thanks all the same."

"All right. See you in the morning. Give you a gull breakfast."

The farmer grinned and turned his car to the farm entrance.

Nat hurried on. Past the little wood, past the old barn, and then across the stile to the remaining field.

As he jumped the stile he heard the whirr of wings. A black-backed gull dived down at him from the sky, missed, swerved in flight, and rose to dive again. In a moment it was joined by others, six, seven, a dozen, black-backed and herring mixed. Nat dropped his hoe. The hoe was useless. Covering his head with his arms he ran towards the cottage. They kept coming at him from the air, silent save for the beating wings. The terrible, fluttering wings. He could feel the blood on his hands, his wrists, his neck. Each stab of a swooping beak tore his flesh. If only he could keep them from his eyes. Nothing else mattered. He must keep them from his eyes. They had not learnt yet how to cling to a shoulder, how to rip clothing, how to dive in mass upon the head, upon the body. But with each dive, with each attack, they became bolder. And they had no thought for themselves. When they dived low and missed, they crashed, bruised and broken, on the ground. As Nat ran he stumbled, kicking their spent bodies in front of him.

He found the door, he hammered upon it with his bleeding hands. Because of the boarded windows no light shone. Everything was dark.

"Let me in," he shouted, "it's Nat. Let me in."

He shouted loud to make himself heard above the whirr of the gull's wings.

Then he saw the gannet, poised for the dive, above him in the sky. The gulls circled, retired, soared, one with another, against the wind. Only the gannet remained. One single gannet, above him in the sky. The wings folded suddenly to its body. It dropped, like a stone. Nat screamed, and the door opened. He stumbled across the threshold, and his wife threw her weight against the door.

They heard the thud of the gannet as it fell.

His wife dressed his wounds. They were not deep. The backs of his hands had suffered most, and his wrists. Had he not worn a cap they would have reached his head. As to the gannet . . . the gannet could have split his skull.

The children were crying, of course. They had seen the blood on their father's hands.

"It's all right now," he told them. "I'm not hurt. Just a few scratches. You play with Johnny, Jill. Mammy will wash these cuts."

He half shut the door to the scullery, so that they could not see. His wife was ashen. She began running water from the sink.

"I saw them overhead," she whispered. "They began collecting just as Jill ran in with Mr Trigg. I shut the door fast, and it jammed. That's why I couldn't open it at once, when you came."

"Thank God they waited for me," he said. "Jill would have fallen at once. One bird alone would have done it."

Furtively, so as not to alarm the children, they whispered together, as she bandaged his hands and the back of his neck.

"They're flying inland," he said, "thousands of them. Rooks, crows, all the bigger birds. I saw them from the bus-stop. They're making for the towns."

"But what can they do, Nat?"

"They'll attack. Go for everyone out in the streets. Then they'll try the windows, the chimneys."

"Why don't the authorities do something? Why don't they get the army, get machine-guns, anything?"

"There's been no time. Nobody's prepared. We'll hear what they have to say on the six o'clock news."

Nat went back into the kitchen, followed by his wife. Johnny was playing quietly on the floor. Only Jill looked anxious.

"I can hear the birds," she said. "Listen, Dad."

Nat listened. Muffled sounds came from the windows, from the door. Wings brushing the surface, sliding, scraping, seeking a way of entry. The sound of many bodies, pressed together, shuffling on the sills. Now and again came a thud, a crash, as some bird dived and fell. "Some of them will kill themselves that way," he thought, "but not enough. Never enough."

"All right," he said aloud, "I've got boards over the windows, Jill. The birds can't get in."

He went and examined all the windows. His work had been thorough. Every gap was closed. He would make extra certain, however. He found wedges, pieces of old tin, strips of wood and metal, and fastened them at the sides to reinforce the boards. His hammering helped to deafen the sound of the birds, the shuffling, the tapping, and more ominous – he did not want his wife or the children to hear it – the splinter of cracked glass.

"Turn on the wireless," he said, "let's have the wireless."

This would drown the sound also. He went upstairs to the bedrooms and reinforced the windows there. Now he could hear the birds on the roof, the scraping of claws, a sliding, jostling sound.

He decided they must sleep in the kitchen, keep up the fire, bring down the mattresses and lay them out on the floor. He was afraid of the bedroom chimneys. The boards he had placed at the chimney bases might give way. In the kitchen they would be safe, because of the fire. He would have to make a joke of it. Pretend to the children they were playing at camp. If the worst happened, and the birds forced an entry down the bedroom chimneys, it would be hours, days perhaps, before they could break down the doors. The birds would be imprisoned in the bedrooms. They could do no harm there. Crowded together, they would stifle and die.

He began to bring the mattresses downstairs. At sight of them his wife's eyes widened in apprehension. She thought the birds had already broken in upstairs.

"All right," he said cheerfully, "we'll all sleep together in the kitchen tonight. More cosy here by the fire. Then we shan't be worried by those silly old birds tapping at the windows."

He made the childen help him rearrange the furniture, and he took the precaution of moving the dresser, with his wife's help, across the window. It fitted well. It was an added safeguard. The mattresses could now be lain, one beside the other, against the wall where the dresser had stood.

"We're safe enough now," he thought, "we're snug and tight, like an air-raid shelter. We can hold out. It's just the food that worries me. Food, and coal for the fire. We've enough for two or three days, not more. By that time . . ."

No use thinking ahead as far as that. And they'd be giving directions on the wireless. People would be told what to do. And now, in the midst of many problems, he realized that it was dance music only coming over the air. Not Children's Hour, as it should have been. He glanced at the dial. Yes, they were on the Home Service all right. Dance records. He switched to the Light programme. He knew the reason. The usual programmes had been abandoned. This only happened at exceptional times. Elections, and such. He tried to remember if it had happened in the war, during the heavy raids on London. But of course. The B.B.C. was not stationed in London during the war. The programmes were broadcast from other, temporary quarters. "We're better off here," he thought, "we're better off here in the kitchen, with the windows and the doors boarded, than they are up in the towns. Thank God we're not in the towns."

At six o'clock the records ceased. The time signal was given. No matter if it scared the children, he must hear the news. There was a pause after the pips. Then the announcer spoke. His voice was solemn, grave. Quite different from midday.

"This is London," he said. "A National Emergency was proclaimed at four o'clock this afternoon. Measures are being taken to safeguard the lives and property of the population, but it must be understood that these are not easy to effect immediately, owing to the unforeseen and unparalleled nature of the present crisis. Every householder must take precautions to his own building, and where several people live together, as in flats and apartments, they must unite to do the utmost they can to prevent entry. It is absolutely imperative that every individual stays indoors tonight, and that no one at all remains on the streets, or roads, or anywhere without doors. The birds, in vast numbers, are attacking anyone on sight, and have already begun an assault upon buildings; but these, with due care, should be impenetrable. The population is asked to remain calm, and not to panic. Owing to the exceptional nature of the emergency, there will be no further transmission from any broadcasting station until seven a.m. tomorrow."

They played the National Anthem. Nothing more happened. Nat switched off the set. He looked at his wife. She stared back at him.

"What's it mean?" said Jill. "What did the news say?"

"There won't be any more programmes tonight," said Nat. "There's been a breakdown at the B.B.C."

"Is it the birds?" asked Jill. "Have the birds done it?"

"No," said Nat, "it's just that everyone's very busy, and then of course they have to get rid of the birds, messing everything up, in the towns. Well, we can manage without the wireless for one evening."

"I wish we had a gramophone," said Jill, "that would be better than nothing."

She had her face turned to the dresser, backed against the windows. Try as they did to ignore it, they were all aware of the shuffling, the stabbing, the persistent beating and sweeping of wings.

"We'll have supper early," suggested Nat, "something for a treat. Ask Mammy. Toasted cheese, eh? Something we all like?"

He winked and nodded at his wife. He wanted the look of dread, of apprehension, to go from Jill's face.

He helped with the supper, whistling, singing, making as much clatter as he could, and it seemed to him that the shuffling and the tapping were not so intense as they had been at first. Presently he went up to the bedrooms and listened, and he no longer heard the jostling for place upon the roof.

"They've got reasoning powers," he thought, "they know it's hard to break in here. They'll try elsewhere. They won't waste their time with us."

Supper passed without incident, and then, when they were clearing away, they heard a new sound, droning, familiar, a sound they all knew and understood.

His wife looked up at him, her face alight. "It's planes," she said, "they're sending out planes after the birds. That's what I said they ought to do, all along. That will get them. Isn't that gun-fire? Can't you hear guns?"

It might be gun-fire, out at sea. Nat could not tell. Big naval guns might have an effect upon the gulls out at sea, but the gulls were inland now. The guns couldn't shell the shore, because of the population.

"It's good, isn't it," said his wife, "to hear the planes?"

And Jill, catching her enthusiasm, jumped up and down with Johnny. "The planes will get the birds. The planes will shoot them."

Just then they heard a crash about two miles distant, followed by a second, then a third. The droning became more distant, passed away out to sea.

"What was that?" asked his wife. "Were they dropping bombs on the birds?"

"I don't know," answered Nat, "I don't think so."

He did not want to tell her that the sound they had heard was the crashing of aircraft. It was, he had no doubt, a venture on the part of the authorities to send out reconnaissance forces, but they might have known the venture was suicidal. What could aircraft do against birds that flung themselves to death against propeller and fuselage, but hurtle to the ground themselves? This was being tried now, he supposed, over the whole country. And at a cost.

Someone high up had lost his head.

"Where have the planes gone, Dad?" asked Jill.

"Back to base," he said. "Come on, now, time to tuck down for bed."

It kept his wife occupied, undressing the children before the fire, seeing to the bedding, one thing and another, while he went round the cottage again, making sure that nothing had worked loose. There was no further drone of aircraft, and the naval guns had ceased. "Waste of life and effort," Nat said to himself. "We can't destroy enough of them that way. Cost too heavy. There's always gas. Maybe they'll try spraying with gas, mustard gas. We'll be warned first, of course, if they do. There's one thing, the best brains of the country will be on to it tonight."

Somehow the thought reassured him. He had a picture of scientists, naturalists, technicians, and all those chaps they called the back-room boys, summoned to a council; they'd be working on the problem now. This was not a job for the government, for the chiefs-of-staff – they would merely carry out the orders of the scientists.

"They'll have to be ruthless," he thought. "Where the trouble's worst they'll have to risk more lives, if they use gas. All the livestock, too, and the soil – all contaminated. As long as everyone doesn't panic. That's the trouble. People panicking, losing their heads. The B.B.C. was right to warn us of that."

Upstairs in the bedrooms all was quiet. No further scraping and stabbing at the windows. A lull in battle. Forces regrouping. Wasn't that what they called it, in the old war-time bulletins? The wind hadn't dropped, though. He could still hear it, roaring in the chimneys. And the sea breaking down on the shore. Then he remembered the tide. The tide would be on the turn. Maybe the lull in battle was because of the tide. There was some law the birds obeyed, and it was all to do with the east wind and the tide.

He glanced at his watch. Nearly eight o'clock. It must have gone high water an hour ago. That explained the lull: the birds attacked with the flood tide. It might not work that way inland, up country, but it seemed as if it was so this way on the coast. He reckoned the time limit in his head. They had six hours to go, without attack. When the tide turned again, around one-twenty in the morning, the birds would come back. . . .

There were two things he could do. The first to rest, with his wife and the children, and all of them snatch what sleep they could, until the small hours. The second to go out, see how they were faring at the farm, see if the telephone was still working there, so that they might get news from the exchange.

He called softly to his wife, who had just settled the children. She came half-way up the stairs and he whispered to her.

"You're not to go," she said at once, "you're not to go and leave me alone with the children. I can't stand it."

Her voice rose hysterically. He hushed her, calmed her.

"All right," he said, "all right. I'll wait till morning. And we'll get the wireless bulletin then too, at seven. But in the morning, when the tide ebbs again, I'll try for the farm, and they may let us have bread and potatoes, and milk too."

His mind was busy again, planning against emergency. They would not have milked, of course, this evening. The cows would be standing by the gate, waiting in the yard, with the household inside, battened behind boards, if they were at the cottage. That is, if they had time to take precautions. He thought of the farmer, Trigg, smiling at him from the car. There would have been no shooting party, not tonight.

The children were asleep. His wife, still clothed, was sitting on her mattress. She watched him, her eyes nervous.

"What are you going to do?" she whispered.

He shook his head for silence. Softly, stealthily, he opened the back door and looked outside.

It was pitch dark. The wind was blowing harder than ever, coming in steady gusts, icy, from the sea. He kicked at the step outside the door. It was heaped with birds. There were dead birds everywhere. Under the windows, against the walls. These were the suicides, the divers, the ones with broken necks. Wherever he looked he saw dead birds. No trace of the living. The living had flown seaward with the turn of the tide. The gulls would be riding the seas now, as they had done in the forenoon.

In the far distance, on the hill where the tractor had been two days before, something was burning. One of the aircraft that had crashed; the fire, fanned by the wind, had set light to a stack.

He looked at the bodies of the birds, and he had a notion that if he heaped them, one upon the other, on the window sills they would make added protection for the next attack. Not much, perhaps, but something. The bodies would have to be clawed at, pecked, and dragged aside, before the living birds gained purchase on the sills and attacked the panes. He set to work in the darkness. It was queer; he hated touching them. The bodies were still warm and bloody. The blood matted their feathers. He felt his stomach turn, but he went on with his work. He noticed, grimly, that every window-pane was shattered. Only the boards had kept the birds from breaking in. He stuffed the cracked panes with the bleeding bodies of the birds.

When he had finished he went back into the cottage. He barricaded the kitchen door, made it doubly secure. He took off his bandages, sticky with the birds' blood, not with his own cuts, and put on fresh plaster.

His wife had made him cocoa and he drank it thirstily. He was very tired.

"All right," he said, smiling, "don't worry. We'll get through."

He lay down on his mattress and closed his eyes. He slept at once. He dreamt uneasily, because through his dreams there ran a thread of something forgotten. Some piece of work, neglected, that he should have done. Some precaution that he had known well but had not taken, and he could not put a name to it in his dreams. It was connected in some way with the burning aircraft and the stack upon the hill. He went on sleeping, though; he did not awake. It was his wife shaking his shoulder that awoke him finally.

"They've begun," she sobbed, "they've started this last hour, I can't listen to it any longer, alone. There's something smelling bad too, something burning."

Then he remembered. He had forgotten to make up the fire. It was smouldering, nearly out. He got up swiftly and lit the lamp. The hammering had started at the windows and the doors, but it was not that he minded now. It was the smell of singed feathers. The smell filled the kitchen. He knew at once what it was. The birds were coming down the chimney, squeezing their way down to the kitchen range.

He got sticks and paper and put them on the embers, then reached for the can of paraffin.

"Stand back," he shouted to his wife, "we've got to risk this."

He threw the paraffin on to the fire. The flame roared up the pipe, and down upon the fire fell the scorched, blackened bodies of the birds.

The children woke, crying. "What is it?" said Jill. "What's happened?"

Nat had no time to answer. He was raking the bodies from the chimney, clawing them out on to the floor. The flames still roared, and the danger of the chimney catching fire was one he had to take. The flames would send away the living birds from the chimney top. The lower joint was the difficulty, though. This was choked with the smouldering helpless bodies of the birds caught by fire. He scarcely heeded the attack on the windows and the door: let them beat their wings, break their beaks, lose their lives, in the attempt to force an entry into his home. They would not break in. He thanked God he had one of the old cottages, with small windows, stout walls. Not like the new council houses. Heaven help them up the lane, in the new council houses.

"Stop crying," he called to the children. "There's nothing to be afraid of, stop crying."

He went on raking at the burning, smouldering bodies as they fell into the fire.

"This'll fetch them," he said to himself, "the draught and the flames together. We're all right, as long as the chimney doesn't catch. I ought to be shot for this. It's all my fault. Last thing I should have made up the fire. I knew there was something."

Amid the scratching and tearing at the window boards came the sudden homely striking of the kitchen clock. Three a.m. A little more than four hours yet to go. He could not be sure of the exact time of high water. He reckoned it would not turn much before half past seven, twenty to eight.

"Light up the primus," he said to his wife. "Make us some tea, and the kids some cocoa. No use sitting around doing nothing."

That was the line. Keep her busy, and the children too. Move about, eat, drink; always best to be on the go.

He waited by the range. The flames were dying. But no more blackened bodies fell from the chimney. He thrust his poker up as far as it could go and found nothing. It was clear. The chimney was clear. He wiped the sweat from his forehead.

"Come on now, Jill," he said, "bring me some more sticks. We'll have a good fire going directly." She wouldn't come near him, though. She was staring at the heaped singed bodies of the birds.

"Never mind them," he said, "we'll put those in the passage when I've got the fire steady."

The danger of the chimney was over. It could not happen again, not if the fire was kept burning day and night.

"I'll have to get more fuel from the farm tomorrow," he thought. "This will never last. I'll manage, though. I can do all that with the ebb tide. It can be worked, fetching what we need, when the tide's turned. We've just got to adapt ourselves, that's all."

They drank tea and cocoa and ate slices of bread and Bovril. Only half a loaf left, Nat noticed. Never mind though, they'd get by.

"Stop it," said young Johnny, pointing to the windows with his spoon, "stop it, you old birds."

"That's right," said Nat, smiling, "we don't want the old beggars, do we? Had enough of 'em."

They began to cheer when they heard the thud of the suicide birds.

"There's another, Dad," cried Jill, "he's done for."

"He's had it," said Nat, "there he goes, the blighter."

This was the way to face up to it. This was the spirit. If they could keep this up, hang on like this until seven, when the first news bulletin came through, they would not have done too badly.

"Give us a fag," he said to his wife. "A bit of a smoke will clear away the smell of the scorched feathers."

"There's only two left in the packet," she said. "I was going to buy you some from the Co-op."

"I'll have one," he said, "t'other will keep for a rainy day."

No sense trying to make the children rest. There was no rest to be got while the tapping and the scratching went on at the windows. He sat with one arm round his wife and the other round Jill, with Johnny on his mother's lap and the blankets heaped about them on the mattress.

"You can't help admiring the beggars," he said, "they've got persistence. You'd think they'd tire of the game, but not a bit of it."

Admiration was hard to sustain. The tapping went on and on and a new rasping note struck Nat's ear, as though a sharper beak than any hitherto had come to take over from its fellows. He tried to remember the names of birds, he tried to think which species would go for this particular job. It was not the tap of the woodpecker. That would be light and frequent. This was more serious, because if it continued long the wood would splinter as the glass had done. Then he remembered the hawks. Could the hawks have taken over from the gulls? Were there buzzards now upon the sills, using talons as well as beaks? Hawks, buzzards, kestrels, falcons – he had forgotten the birds of prey. He had forgotten the gripping power of the birds of prey. Three hours to go, and while they waited the sound of the splintering wood, the talons tearing at the wood.

Nat looked about him, seeing what furniture he could destroy to fortify the door. The windows were safe, because of the dresser. He was not certain of the door. He went upstairs, but when he reached the landing he paused and listened. There was a soft patter on the floor of the children's bedroom. The birds had broken through ... He put his ear to the door. No mistake. He could hear the rustle of wings, and the light patter as they searched the floor. The other bedroom was still clear. He went into it and began bringing out the furniture, to pile at the head of the stairs should the door of the children's bedroom go. It was a preparation. It might never be needed. He could not stack the furniture against the door, because it opened inward. The only possible thing was to have it at the top of the stairs.

"Come down, Nat, what are you doing?" called his wife.

"I won't be long," he shouted. "Just making everything shipshape up here."

He did not want her to come; he did not want her to hear the pattering of the feet in the children's bedroom, the brushing of those wings against the door.

At five-thirty he suggested breakfast, bacon and fried bread, if only to stop the growing look of panic in his wife's eyes and to calm the fretful children. She did not know about the birds upstairs. The bedroom, luckily, was not over the kitchen. Had it been so she could not have failed to hear the sound of them, up there, tapping the boards. And the silly, senseless thud of the suicide birds, the death-and-glory boys, who flew into the bedroom, smashing their heads against the walls. He knew them of old, the herring gulls. They had no brains. The black-backs were different, they knew what they were doing. So did the buzzards, the hawks. ...

He found himself watching the clock, gazing at the hands that went so slowly round the dial. If his theory was not correct, if the attack did not cease with the turn of the tide, he knew they were beaten. They could not continue through the long day without air, without rest, without more fuel, without ... his mind raced. He knew there were so many things they needed to withstand siege. They were not fully prepared. They were not ready. It might be that it would be safer in the towns after all. If he could get a message through, on the farm telephone, to his cousin, only a short journey by train up country they might be able to hire a car. That would be quicker – hire a car between tides. ...

His wife's voice, calling his name, drove away the sudden, desperate desire for sleep.

"What is it? What now?" he said sharply.

"The wireless," said his wife. "I've been watching the clock. It's nearly seven."

"Don't twist the knob," he said, impatient for the first time, "it's on the Home where it is. They'll speak from the Home."

They waited. The kitchen clock struck seven. There was no sound. No chimes, no music. They waited until a quarter past, switching to the Light. The result was the same. No news bulletin came through.

"We've heard wrong," he said, "they won't be broadcasting until eight o'clock."

They left it switched on, and Nat thought of the battery, wondered how much power was left in it. It was generally recharged when his wife went shopping in the town. If the battery failed they would not hear the instructions.

"It's getting light," whispered his wife, "I can't see it, but I can feel it. And the birds aren't hammering so loud."

She was right. The rasping, tearing sound grew fainter every moment. So did the shuffling, the jostling for place upon the step, upon the sills. The tide was on the turn. By eight there was no sound at all. Only the wind. The children, lulled at last by the stillness, fell asleep. At half past eight Nat switched the wireless off.

"What are you doing? We'll miss the news," said his wife.

"There isn't going to be any news," said Nat. "We've got to depend upon ourselves."

He went to the door and slowly pulled away the barricades. He drew the bolts, and kicking the bodies from the step outside the door breathed the cold air. He had six working hours before him, and he knew he must reserve his strength for the right things, not waste it in any way. Food, and light, and fuel; these were the necessary things. If he could get them in sufficiency, they could endure another night.

He stepped into the garden, and as he did so he saw the living birds. The gulls had gone to ride the sea, as they had done before; they sought sea food, and the buoyancy of the tide, before they returned to the attack. Not so the land birds. They waited and watched. Nat saw them, on the hedgerows, on the soil, crowded in the trees, outside in the field, line upon line of birds, all still, doing nothing.

He went to the end of his small garden. The birds did not move. They went on watching him.

"I've got to get food," said Nat to himself, "I've got to go to the farm to find food."

He went back to the cottage. He saw to the windows and the doors. He went upstairs and opened the children's bedroom. It was empty, except for the dead birds on the floor. The living were out there, in the garden, in the fields. He went downstairs.

"I'm going to the farm," he said.

His wife clung to him. She had seen the living birds from the open door.

"Take us with you," she begged, "we can't stay here alone. I'd rather die than stay here alone."

He considered the matter. He nodded.

"Come on, then," he said, "bring baskets, and Johnny's pram. We can load up the pram."

They dressed against the biting wind, wore gloves and scarves. His wife put Johnny in the pram. Nat took Jill's hand.

"The birds," she whimpered, "they're all out there, in the fields."

"They won't hurt us," he said, "not in the light."

They started walking across the field towards the stile, and the birds did not move. They waited, their heads turned to the wind.

When they reached the turning to the farm, Nat stopped and told his wife to wait in the shelter of the hedge with the two children.

"But I want to see Mrs Trigg," she protested. "There are lots of things we can borrow, if they went to market yesterday; not only bread, and . . ."

"Wait here," Nat interrupted. "I'll be back in a moment."

The cows were lowing, moving restlessly in the yard, and he could see a gap in the fence where the sheep had knocked their way through, to roam unchecked in the front garden before the farm-house. No smoke came from the chimneys. He was filled with misgiving. He did not want his wife or the children to go down to the farm.

"Don't jib now," said Nat, harshly, "do what I say."

She withdrew with the pram into the hedge, screening herself and the children from the wind.

He went down alone to the farm. He pushed his way through the herd of bellowing cows, which turned this way and that, distressed, their udders full. He saw the car standing by the gate, not put away in the garage. The windows of the farm-house were smashed. There were many dead gulls lying in the yard and around the house. The living birds perched on the group of trees behind the farm and on the roof of the house. They were quite still. They watched him.

Jim's body lay in the yard . . . what was left of it. When the birds had finished, the cows had trampled him. His gun was beside him. The door of the house was shut and bolted, but as the windows were smashed it was easy to lift them and climb through. Trigg's body was close to the telephone. He must have been trying to get through to the exchange when the birds came for him. The receiver was hanging loose, the instrument torn from the wall. No sign of Mrs Trigg. She would be upstairs. Was it any use going up? Sickened, Nat knew what he would find.

"Thank God," he said to himself, "there were no children."

He forced himself to climb the stairs, but half-way he turned and descended again. He could see her legs, protruding from the open bedroom door. Beside her were the bodies of the black-backed gulls, and an umbrella, broken.

"It's no use," thought Nat, "doing anything. I've only got five hours, less than that. The Triggs would understand. I must load up with what I can find."

He tramped back to his wife and children.

"I'm going to fill up the car with stuff," he said. "I'll put coal in it, and paraffin for the primus. We'll take it home and return for a fresh load."

"What about the Triggs?" asked his wife.

"They must have gone to friends," he said.

"Shall I come and help you, then?"

"No; there's a mess down there. Cows and sheep all over the place. Wait, I'll get the car. You can sit in it."

Clumsily he backed the car out of the yard and into the lane. His wife and the children could not see Jim's body from there.

"Stay here," he said, "never mind the pram. The pram can be fetched later. I'm going to load the car."

Her eyes watched his all the time. He believed she understood, otherwise she would have suggested helping him to find the bread and groceries.

They made three journeys altogether, backwards and forwards between their cottage and the farm, before he was satisfied they had everything they needed. It was surprising, once he started thinking, how many things were necessary. Almost the most important of all was planking for the windows. He had to go round searching for timber. He wanted to renew the boards on all the windows at the cottage. Candles, paraffin, nails, tinned stuff; the list was endless. Besides all that, he milked three of the cows. The rest, poor brutes, would have to go on bellowing.

On the final journey he drove the car to the bus-stop, got out, and went to the telephone box. He waited a few minutes, jangling the receiver. No good, though. The line was dead. He climbed on to a bank and looked over the countryside, but there was no sign of life at all, nothing in the fields but the waiting, watching birds. Some of them slept – he could see the beaks tucked into the feathers.

"You'd think they'd be feeding," he said to himself, "not just standing in that way."

Then he remembered. They were gorged with food. They had eaten their fill during the night. That was why they did not move this morning. . . .

No smoke came from the chimneys of the council houses. He thought of the children who had run across the fields the night before.

"I should have known," he thought, "I ought to have taken them home with me."

He lifted his face to the sky. It was colourless and grey. The bare trees on the landscape looked bent and blackened by the east wind. The cold did not affect the living birds, waiting out there in the fields.

"This is the time they ought to get them," said Nat, "they're a sitting target now. They must be doing this all over the country. Why don't our aircraft take off now and spray them with mustard gas? What are all our chaps doing? They must know, they must see for themselves."

He went back to the car and got into the driver's seat.

"Go quickly past that second gate," whispered his wife. "The postman's lying there. I don't want Jill to see."

He accelerated. The little Morris bumped and rattled along the lane. The children shrieked with laughter.

"Up-a-down, up-a-down," shouted young Johnny.

It was a quarter to one by the time they reached the cottage. Only an hour to go.

"Better have cold dinner," said Nat. "Hot up something for yourself and the children, some of that soup. I've no time to eat now. I've got to unload all this stuff."

He got everything inside the cottage. It could be sorted later. Give them all something to do during the long hours ahead. First he must see to the windows and the doors.

He went round the cottage methodically, testing every window, every door. He climbed on to the roof also, and fixed boards across every chimney, except the kitchen. The cold was so intense he could hardly bear it, but the job had to be done. Now and again he would look up, searching the sky for aircraft. None came. As he worked he cursed the inefficiency of the authorities.

"It's always the same," he muttered, "they always let us down. Muddle, muddle, from the start. No plan, no real organization. And we don't matter, down here. That's what it is. The people up country have priority. They're using gas up there, no doubt, and all the aircraft. We've got to wait and take what comes."

He paused, his work on the bedroom chimney finished, and looked out to sea. Something was moving out there. Something grey and white amongst the breakers.

"Good old Navy," he said, "they never let us down. They're coming down channel, they're turning in the bay."

He waited, straining his eyes, watering in the wind, towards the sea. He was wrong, though. It was not ships. The Navy was not there. The gulls were rising from the sea. The massed flocks in the fields, with ruffled feathers, rose in formation from the ground, and wing to wing soared upwards to the sky.

The tide had turned again.

Nat climbed down the ladder and went inside the kitchen. The family were at dinner. It was a little after two. He bolted the door, put up the barricade, and lit the lamp.

"It's night-time," said young Johnny.

His wife had switched on the wireless once again, but no sound came from it.

"I've been all round the dial," she said, "foreign stations, and that lot. I can't get anything."

"Maybe they have the same trouble," he said, "maybe it's the same right through Europe."

She poured out a plateful of the Triggs' soup, cut him a large slice of the Triggs' bread, and spread their dripping upon it.

They ate in silence. A piece of the dripping ran down young Johnny's chin and fell on to the table.

"Manners, Johnny," said Jill, "you should learn to wipe your mouth."

The tapping began at the windows, at the door. The rustling, the jostling, the pushing for position on the sills. The first thud of the suicide gulls upon the step.

"Won't America do something?" said his wife. "They've always been our allies, haven't they? Surely America will do something?"

Nat did not answer. The boards were strong against the windows, and on the chimneys too. The cottage was filled with stores, with fuel, with all they needed for the next few days. When he had finished dinner he would put the stuff away, stack it neatly, get everything shipshape, handy-like. His wife could help him, and the children too. They'd tire themselves out, between now and a quarter to nine, when the tide would ebb; then he'd tuck them down on their mattresses, see that they slept good and sound until three in the morning.

He had a new scheme for the windows, which was to fix barbed wire in front of the boards. He had brought a great roll of it from the farm. The nuisance was, he'd have to work at this in the dark, when the lull came between nine and three. Pity he had not thought of it before. Still, as long as the wife slept, and the kids, that was the main thing.

The smaller birds were at the window now. He recognized the light tap-tapping of their beaks, and the soft brush of their wings. The hawks ignored the windows. They concentrated their attack upon the door. Nat listened to the tearing sound of splintering wood, and wondered how many million years of memory were stored in those little brains, behind the stabbing beaks, the piercing eyes, now giving them this instinct to destroy mankind with all the deft precision of machines.

"I'll smoke that last fag," he said to his wife. "Stupid of me, it was the one thing I forgot to bring back from the farm."

He reached for it, switched on the silent wireless. He threw the empty packet on the fire, and watched it burn.

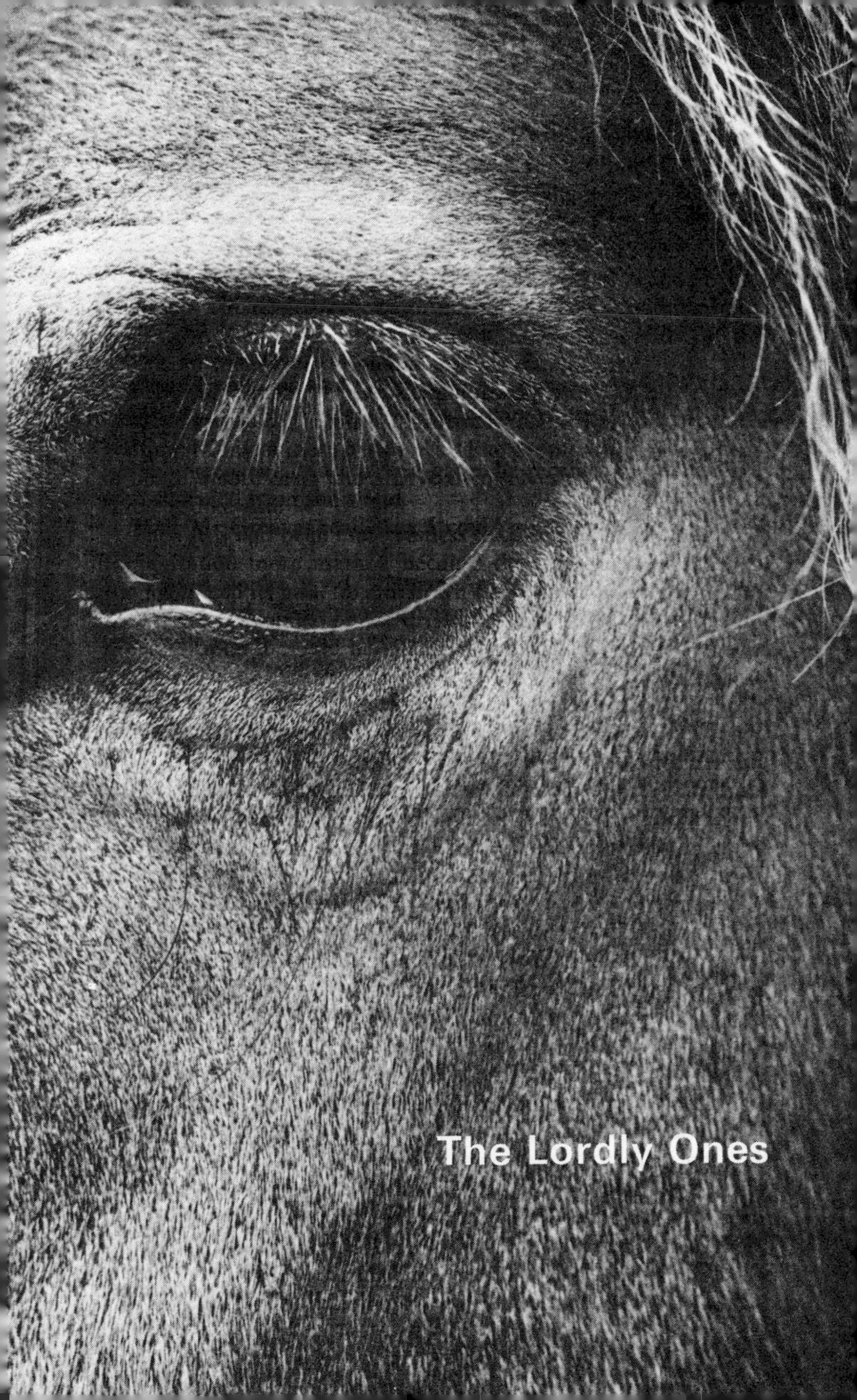

The Lordly Ones

The Lordly Ones

Ben was thought to be backward. He could not speak. When he tried to form words sounds came, harsh and ugly, and he did not know what to do with his tongue. He pointed when he wanted something, or fetched it for himself. They said he was tongue-tied, and that in a few years' time he would be taken to hospital and something could be done. His mother said he was sharp enough, he took in what you told him all right, and knew good from bad, but he was stubborn, he did not take kindly to "no". Because of his silence they forgot to explain things to him, arrivals and departures and changes of plan, and his world was made up of whims, the whims of older people. He would be told to dress for no reason, or to go out into the street to play; or some toy was denied him that had been given him an hour before.

When the stress became too great to bear he opened his mouth, and the sound that came out of it alarmed him even more than it alarmed his parents. Why did it rise? How did it come? Then someone, usually his mother, picked him up and shut him away in the cupboard under the stairs, amongst the mackintoshes and the shopping baskets, and he could hear her calling through the keyhole, "You'll stop there until you're quiet!" The noise would not be quelled. It did not belong to him. The anger was a force that had to have its way.

Later, crouched beside the keyhole, spent and tired, he would hear the noise die away, and peace would come to the cupboard. The fear would then be that his mother would go away and forget to let him out, and he would rattle the handle of the door to remind her. A flash of her skirt through the keyhole meant reassurance, and he would sit down and wait until the grinding of the key in the lock spelt release. Then he would step out into the daylight, blinking, and glance up at his mother to gauge her mood. If she was dusting or sweeping, she ignored him. All would be well until the next moment of anger or frustration, when the performance would be repeated – either the cupboard again, or his bedroom with no tea, his toys taken from him. The way to ensure against their anger was to please his parents, but this could not always be done, for the strain was too great. In the middle of play, absorbed, he forgot their commands.

One day suitcases were packed and he was dressed in his warmest clothes, although it was early spring, and they left the house in Exeter where he had been born and went to the moors. There had been talk about the moors for some weeks past.

"It's different up there from what it is down here," his parents would say. Somehow cajolery and threats were combined: one day he was to be lucky, another he had better not get out of sight once they moved. The very words "the moors" sounded dark and ominous, a sort of threat.

The bustle of departure added to fear. The rooms of his home, suddenly bare, were unfamiliar, and his mother, impatient, scolded him ceaselessly. She too wore different clothes, and an ugly hat. It clung round her ears, changing the shape of her face. As they left home she seized his hand, dragging it, and bewildered he watched his parents as they sat, anxious themselves, among the boxes and the packing-cases. Could it be that they were uncertain too? That none of them knew where they were going?

The train bore them away, but he could not see out of the windows. He was in the middle seat between his parents, and only the tops of trees told him of country. His mother gave him an orange he did not want. Forgetting caution, he threw it on the floor. She smacked him hard. The smack coincided with a sudden jolt of the train and the darkness of a tunnel, the two combined suggesting the cupboard under the stairs and punishment. He opened his mouth and the cry came from it.

As always, the sound brought panic. His mother shook him and he bit his tongue. The carriage was full of strangers. An old man behind a newspaper frowned. A woman, showing her teeth, offered him a green sweet. No one could be trusted. His cries became louder still and his mother, her face red, picked him up and took him into the rattling corridor. "Will you be quiet?" she shouted. All was confusion. Fatigue seized him, and he crumpled. Rage and fear made him stamp his feet, clad in new brown-laced shoes, adding to the clatter. The sound, coming from his belly, ceased; only the gasp for breath, the stifling sobs, told him that the pain was with him, but for what reason he could not tell.

"He's tired," somebody said.

They were back again in the carriage, and room was made for him by the window. The world outside went past. Houses clustered. He saw a road with cars upon it, and fields, then high banks swaying up and down. With the gradual slowing of the train his parents stood up and began to reach for their belongings. The fluster of departure was with them once again. The train ground to a standstill. Doors opened and clanged, and a porter shouted. They tumbled out on to the platform.

His mother clutched him by the hand and he peered up at her face, and at his father's too, to try and discover from their expressions whether what was happening was customary, expected by them, and if they knew what was to happen now. They climbed into a car, the luggage piled about them, and through the gathering dusk he understood that they were not back again in the town from which they had come, but in open country. The air bit sharp, cool-smelling, and his father turned with a laugh to him and said, "Can you smell the moors?"

The moors. . . . He tried to see from the window of the car, but a suitcase balked his view. His mother and father were talking amongst themselves. "She'll surely have put on a kettle for us, and give us a hand," said his mother; and, "We'll not unpack everything tonight. It will take days to get straight."

"I don't know," said his father. "It's surprising how different it will seem in a small house."

The road twisted, the car swaying at the corners. Ben felt sick. This would be the final disgrace. The sourness was coming and he shut his mouth. But the urge was too strong, and it came from him in a burst, splaying out over the car.

"Oh, no, that's too much," cried his mother, and she pushed him from her knee against the sharp end of the suitcase, bruising his cheek. His father tapped the window. "Stop . . . the boy's been sick." The shame, the inevitable confusion of sickness, and with it the sudden cold so that he shivered. Everywhere lay the evidence of his shame, and an old cloth, evil-smelling, was produced by the driver to wipe his mouth.

On again, but slower now, standing between his father's knees, and at last the rutty, bumpy road came to an end and a light was in front of them.

"It's not raining, that's one blessing," said his mother. "Don't ask me what we'll do here when it does."

The small house stood alone, light in the windows. Ben, blinking and shivering still, climbed down from the car. He stood looking about him as the luggage was lifted out. For the moment he was ignored. The small house faced a green, smooth as a carpet in the dark, and behind the house, which was thatched, were humped black hills. The sharp sweet smell he had noticed on leaving the station was stronger still. He lifted his face to sniff the air. Where were the moors? He saw them as a band of brothers, powerful and friendly.

"Come on in, my handsome," said a woman from the house, and he did not draw back when she bore down upon him, welcoming and large, and led him into the paved kitchen. A stool was drawn up to the table and a glass of milk put in front of him. He sipped it slowly, his eyes sizing up the flagged kitchen, the scullery pump, the small latticed windows.

"Is he shy?" asked the woman, and the whispers began, the grown-up talk, something about his tongue. His father and his mother looked embarrassed and awkward. The woman glanced back again, in pity, and Ben dipped his face in his glass of milk. Then they forgot him, the dull talk passed him by, and unwatched he was able to eat bread and butter without hindrance, help himself to biscuits, his sickness gone and appetite returned.

"Oh yes, watch out for them," the woman said. "They're terrible thieves. They'll come by night and raid your larder, if you leave it open. Especially if it continues cold like this. Watch out for snow."

So the moors were robbers. A band of robbers wandering by night. Ben remembered the comic paper that his father had bought him, with the ogre's face upon the cover. Yet they could not be like that, for the woman was saying something about their fine looks.

"They won't hurt you," she said, "they're friendly enough." This to Ben, who watched her, puzzled. Then she laughed, and everyone got up to clear the tea, to unpack, to settle.

"Now then, don't wander off," said his mother. "If you don't behave you'll go straight to bed."

"He can't come to harm," the woman said. "I've latched the gate."

When they were not looking Ben slipped out of the open door and stood outside. The car that had brought them had disappeared. The silence, so different from the noise of the street at home, was like the silence that came when his parents were not angry. It wrapped itself about him. The little lights winking from the other cottages, away down the green, were distant as stars. He went and rested his chin on the gate, and stared into the peaceful darkness. He felt himself at rest. He had no wish to go indoors, to unpack his toys.

There must be a farm somewhere close, for the smell of manure mixed with the cold air, and a cow lowed from a stall. These discoveries were pleasing to him. Mostly he thought about the moors, the thieves of the night, but somehow they did not frighten him: the reassurance of the woman's smile and the way his parents had laughed showed that the moors were not to be feared. Anyway, it was to come to the moors that they had packed their things and left home. It was this that had been discussed now for so many weeks. "The boy will like the moors," people had said, back at home. "He'll grow strong, up there. There's nothing like the moors for giving appetite."

It was true. Ben had eaten five pieces of bread and butter and three biscuits. Already the band of brothers had shown power. He wondered how close they were to the house, if they lurked, smiling encouragement, beyond those dark humped hills.

A sudden thought occurred to him. If food was put out for the thieves, they would not steal. They would eat it and be thankful. He went back inside the kitchen, and voices from upstairs told him that his parents and their helper were unpacking and out of the way. The table had been cleared, but the tea-things, unwashed, were piled in the scullery. There was a loaf of bread, a cake still uncut, and the remaining biscuits. Ben filled his pockets with the biscuits, and carried the loaf of bread and the cake. He went to the door, and so down the path to the gate. He set the food on the ground, and concentrated upon the task of unfastening the gate. It was easier than he had expected. He lifted the latch and the gate swung back. Then he picked up the loaf and the cake and went out on to the green. The thieves made for the green first, the woman had said. They prowled there, looking for odds and ends, and if nothing tempted them, and no one shouted and drove them away, they would come to the cottages.

Ben walked a few yards on to the green and set out the food. The thieves could not miss it if they came. They would be grateful, and go back to their lair in the black hills well satisfied. Looking back, he could see the figures of his parents moving backwards and forwards in the bedrooms upstairs. He jumped, to try the feel of the grass under his feet, more pleasing than a pavement, and lifted his face once more to feel the air. It came, cold and clean, from the hills. It was as though the moors knew, the thieves knew, that a feast was prepared for them. Ben was happy.

He ran back to the house, and as he did so his mother came downstairs.

"Come on, bed," she said.

Bed? So soon? His face protested, but she was not to be moved.

"There's enough to do without you round my heels," she complained.

She pulled him up the steep little stairway after her, and he saw his own bed, miraculously brought from home, standing in a corner of the small room lit by candlelight. It was close to the window, and his first thought was that he would be able to look out from his bed and watch when the thieves came. This interest kept him quiet while his mother helped him to undress, but she was rougher than usual. Her nails got caught in a button and scratched his skin, and when he whimpered she said sharply. "Oh, be quiet, do." The candle, stuck in a saucer, threw a monster shadow on the ceiling. It flounced his mother's figure to a grotesque shape.

"I'm too tired to wash you tonight," she said. "You'll have to stay dirty."

His father's voice called up the stairs. "What did you do with the bread and the cake?" he called. "I can't find them."

"They're on the scullery table," she answered. "I'll be down in a minute."

Ben realized that his parents would search for the food to put it away. Instinct warned him to make no sound. She finished undressing him, and he went straight to his bed without delay.

"Now I don't want to hear any more from you tonight," she said. "If you make a sound I'll send your father to you."

She went downstairs, taking the candle with her.

Ben was used to darkness, but, even so, the room was unfamiliar. He had not yet had time to learn the shape. Was there a chair? A table? Was it long or square? He lay back in bed biting at the blanket. He heard footsteps underneath his window. Sitting up, he looked between the curtains, and saw the woman who had welcomed them walk down the path, through the gate, and away down the road. She was carrying a lantern. She did not cross the green. The lantern danced as she moved, and soon she was swallowed up in the darkness. Only the bobbing light betrayed her passage.

Ben lay back again in bed, disturbed by the flickering lantern and voices raised in argument below. He heard his mother come upstairs. She threw open the door and stood there, holding the candle, the monstrous shadow behind her.

"Did you touch the tea things?" she said.

Ben made the sound his parents understood as a denial, but his mother was not satisfied. She came to the bed and, shielding her eyes, stared down at him.

"The bread and cake have gone," she said. "The biscuits too. You took them, didn't you? Where did you hide them?"

As always, the rising voice brought out antagonism. Ben shrank against his pillow and shut his eyes. It was not the way to question him. If she had smiled and made a joke of it, it would have been different.

"Very well," she said. "I'll settle you, young man."

She called for his father. Despair seized Ben. It would mean a whipping. He began to cry. Explanation was beyond him. He heard his father stump up the stairs and come into the room, his shadow monstrous too. The pair of them filled the small, unfamiliar room.

"Do you want a hiding?" his father asked. "Now then, what did you do with the bread?"

His father's face was ugly, worn with fatigue. The packing and unpacking, all the hustle of removal, of starting the new life, had meant strain. Ben sensed this, but he could not give way. He opened his mouth and yelled. The cry roused the full fatigue and anger of the father. Resentment, too. Why must his son be dumb?

"That's enough of that," he said.

He jerked Ben out of bed and stripped the pyjama legs. Then he laid the wriggling child across his knee. The hand found the flesh and hit hard, with all its force. Ben screamed louder still. The relentless hand, so large and powerful, smote and smote again.

"That's learned him, that's enough," said his mother. "There's neighbours across the green. We don't want trouble."

"He must know who's master," said his father, and it was not until his own hand ached with the force of the blows that he gave up and pushed Ben from his knee.

"Now holler if you dare," he said, rising abruptly, and Ben, face downwards on the bed, his sobs long ceased, heard them withdraw, felt the candle go, knew that the room was empty. Everything was pain. He tried to move his legs, but the movement sent a warning message to his brain. The pain travelled from his buttocks up his spine to the top of his head. No sound came from his lips now, only a trickle of tears from his eyes. Perhaps if he lay quite still the pain would go. He could not cover himself with the blanket, and the cold air found him, bringing its own dull ache.

Little by little the pain numbed. The tears dried on his cheeks. He had no thoughts at all, lying there on his face. He had forgotten the cause of his beating. He had forgotten the band of brothers, the thieves, the moors. If in a little while there could be nothing, let nothing come.

2

He awoke suddenly, every sense alert. The moon shone through the gap in the curtains. At first he thought that everything was still, and the movement from the green outside told him they were there. They had come. He knew. Slowly, painfully, he dragged himself across his bed and so to the window. He pulled at the curtains. The white night showed him the wonder. The thieves were there, the lordly ones. Not as the woman had described them, but more beautiful. A little group, intent upon his offering. There was the mother, with two children, and another mother just behind, with a taller child, playing by himself. Two others ran round in circles, delighting in the snow, for with them the snow had come, turning the green white. That must be the father, watching. But he was not angry, like Ben's father: he was beautiful like the mothers and the children, beautiful and wise. He was staring at the window. He had already seen Ben, and then, to show his appreciation of the cake placed ready for him, he touched it gently and moved away, letting the son play with it instead.

It was the time of night when no one moves. Ben knew nothing of time, but instinct told him that his parents had long been in bed, and that morning would not come for many hours. He watched them, the moors, the lordly ones. They were not thieves at all, they were far too proud. They ate with delicacy what Ben had given them, and they did not attempt to come near to the house, or prowl, as the woman had said. Like Ben, they did not speak. They talked by signal. The father, in command, moved his head, and leaving the food the mothers summoned their children, and the whole company settled themselves on the green, in the snow, to wait for morning. Their supreme disdain of the sleeping houses showed itself to Ben as contempt of authority. They made their own laws.

Ben lowered himself from his bed. His buttocks and back were still very sore, and the cold night had stiffened him, lying as he had done without a cover. Nevertheless, he began to put on his clothes. He dressed slowly, not yet accustomed to doing it quite alone, but finally he satisfied himself that he was ready, although his jersey was back to front. Luckily his wellington boots were in the scullery. They had been among the first things to be unpacked.

He could see his room clearly now, for the moonlight turned it to day. There were no strange bulges or shapes. It was just a room, small and plain. The door-latch was high above his head, so he dragged a chair beneath it and stood on it to lift the latch.

Cunningly he crept down the narrow stair. Below in the kitchen it was still dark, but instinct led him to the scullery, and to the corner where his boots waited. He put them on. The larder was only a cupboard, part of the scullery, and the door was ajar. His mother, in her anger, must have forgotten to close it. Deliberately he took the last loaf, intended for breakfast, and then repeated his performance with the chair beneath the latch of the front door. There were bolts here too to be withdrawn. If his parents heard him, he was lost. He climbed down from the chair. The door lay open. The white night was before him, the great moon benign, and the lordly ones were waiting on the green. It was green no longer, but glistening white.

Softly, his boots lightly crunching the snow, Ben tiptoed down the path and lifted the latch of the gate. The sound roused the watchers on the green. One of the mothers looked up, and although she said nothing her movement warned the father, and he too turned his head. They waited to see what Ben would do. Perhaps, thought Ben, they hoped for further gifts: they had not brought food with them, and were hungry still.

He walked slowly towards them, holding out the loaf. The mother rose to her feet, and the children too. The action roused the others, and in a moment the little company, who had settled themselves for sleep, seemed ready to march once more. They did not try to take the bread from Ben. Some sense of delicacy, perhaps, forbade it. He wanted to show generosity to them and to flaunt his parents at the same time, so, tearing the loaf in two, he went to the smallest child, not much taller than himself, and offered him part of it. This surely would be understood.

The little moor came forward and took the bread, watching Ben when he had eaten it, and then he shook his hair out of his eyes, for he was wild and unkempt, and glanced at his mother. She did not do anything, she did not speak to him, and Ben, encouraged, offered her the other half of the loaf. She took it from him. Their silence pleased Ben, for it was something he understood and shared with them.

The mother had gold hair, like her ragged son, but the older boy was dark. Relationships were confusing, because there was another mother – or could it be an aunt? – who was standing quite close to the father, and a little apart, not taking much notice of anyone, was surely the gran, so grey and thin, who looked as if she did not care for the snow, but would have been more at her ease before a good warm fire. Ben wondered at their roaming ways. What made them wander, rather than stay at home? They were not thieves, he was sure they were not thieves.

Then the father gave a signal. He turned, and slowly, majestically, led the way down the green. The others followed, the children dancing, glad to be on the move again, and the old gran, hobbling, brought up the rear. Ben watched them, then glanced back at the sleeping house. Decision came to him. He was not going to stay with the parents who did not love him. He was going to follow the moors, the lordly ones.

Ben ran across the crunching snow in the wake of his chosen companions. The old gran looked over her shoulder as she heard him coming, but she did not mind. She seemed to accept him. Ben ran until he caught up with the mother he liked best, the one with the golden hair and the ragged son, and when he was beside her she gave him a friendly nod of the head to show that he was now of the company. Ben trudged beside her in the snow. The father, still in front, was making for the hills, but he had a fine instinct for avoiding the deeper snow. He picked his way along a track, drifts on either side, and came at last to a high ridge where the world stretched wide and far on either side. The green was a long way below. Soon it was lost to sight. There were no houses in this wild country, lit by moonlight. Ben was warm from his climb, and so were his companions. Their breath went from them all like smoke in the frosted air.

What now? They looked to the father for instructions. He seemed to debate the move within himself. He glanced to right and to left. Then he decided to continue along the ridge, and once more led the way, with the family following.

The children dragged a little, for they were getting tired, and Ben, to encourage them, jumped and skipped, forgetting his bruised, stiff back. The pain made him cry out, and the cry startled the golden mother, who, staring at him, spoke to him. Was she asking a question? Ben did not understand her language.

He thought that the noises in his throat must have told the mother that his back was stiff, for she seemed reassured and slowed her walk to his. Ben was relieved. He did not want to have to hobble in the rear with the old gran.

Presently the ridge sloped to an old trackway, banked high on either side with snow, and the father stopped here, making as though to camp. He stared across the wastes to the line of distant hills, and did not move. He must be thinking very deeply, decided Ben; he did not want to talk to the others. The mothers wandered around in circles, and then found a resting-place for the children on firm ground against a bank of frozen snow. The old gran, discontented, could not settle. She found the night air cold. Ben wondered what he should do. His legs were aching and he was as tired as the gran. He watched the children curl up in a patch of snow. If they can do that, he thought to himself, I suppose I can too. But they are used to sleeping on the ground, and I am not.

Then the mother, the one he liked, decided to settle by her son. Her broad, comfortable body reminded Ben of the woman who had welcomed him and his parents the night before at the thatched house on the green. She had been kindly too. But this mother was beautiful, more beautiful by far than his own mother. He hesitated a moment, then he crept forward and crouched against her. Would she be angry? Would she push him away?

She did not look at him. She did not speak. She let him understand that he could lie there, against her, and receive her warmth. Her good body smell was comforting. He snuggled close, his head against her shoulder, and put up his hand to touch her hair. She shook her head gently, and sighed. Ben closed his eyes, eased by the warmth, the comfort, the tender understanding of the mother and the reassurance of the father, still watching the far hills. He was the guardian of his sons, he would never beat them. They were all of one company, these moors, not the band of brothers he had imagined, but a family, a tribe, belonging one to the other. He would never leave them, the lordly ones.

3

The sun came over the hills in splendour, and Ben opened his eyes. In a moment it was broad day. Already the old gran was on the move, hobbling about on her stiff legs. Her example put the others to shame, and they rose in turn, the children reluctantly, for they could have done with an hour or two more of sleep. No one had breakfast, and Ben was hungry. What was to be done about food? The bread he had brought with him had all been finished on the green. Uneasily, he remembered that the woman had called them thieves. Perhaps, after all, it was true. They were going to wait until night, and then descend to a village and either beg for bread or steal it. What about the children? Would they last through the day?

Ben stood up and stamped his feet for warmth. Then he stared. The little ragged son, who must surely be of an age with himself, was feeding from his mother. Only babies did that. Was it because the lordly ones were wanderers that they had such wild ways? The mother did not hide herself with her son to do this, as a friend of his own mother's had once done in their back kitchen, but she let it happen now, in the open, with the others looking on. Then abruptly she pushed the small son away, showing him that he had had enough. She began to walk after the father. The long trail started, and Ben stumped along by the mother's side. After all, if it was their custom . . .

He began to wish the mother had fed him too. The ragged son, filled and happy, danced up to him, suggesting play, and Ben, forgetting his hunger, ran after him, laughing, pulling at his hair. They ran in circles, calling to one another. And the ragged son, as he might have done himself, pranced back to tease the gran. He skipped in front of her, mocking the hobbling gait, and nobody minded, thought Ben, nobody told him it was rude.

The sun was high now, the warmth of it melting the snow beneath, and with it came the gnawing pain of hunger in Ben's stomach, and there was nothing to eat, for the lordly ones gave him nothing. Quelling his shyness, he went to the mother and pointed, showing by the sound in his throat that he wanted to feed. She moved away, though, she would not let him. He understood that she kept her food for the son.

They went on walking, they followed the father. He was some way ahead when he suddenly stopped, and, looking back, called to the mothers. They halted, and the mothers returned his cry. Then they waited. Instructions had been given not to move. There was a sound of running in the far distance, and over the hill came another moor, a stranger. He stopped when he saw the father, and the pair of them stared at each other. The mother beside Ben murmured something to her companion, and the company formed a little circle, wondering what the father was going to do.

Ben watched, apprehensive; he did not like the look of the

threatening stranger. The newcomer advanced again, and then, without warning, hurled himself upon the father, and the pair of them wrestled there together in the snow, fiercely, without weapons, the watchful father turning of a sudden to a savage. There was a time of anger, and stamping feet and strangled sobs, and the mothers, watching, huddled together for comfort, Ben in the midst of them. Their fear bred fear in Ben, and he began to cry again, remembering his own angry father. Would the battle never be done? Suddenly it was over. But the result was terror. For the father, the kind leader who had watched over them all night, began to run. Not towards his own family, the mothers and the children, but away across the snow to the distant hills. He was afraid of the stranger. The stranger had defeated him. As Ben watched he saw the trail of blood on the snow.

Ben put out his hand and touched the mother. He tried to tell her that they must follow the wounded father, follow their leader, but she shook herself away impatiently. She was looking at the conqueror. Slowly he advanced towards them. Ben shrank back against the ragged son, as frightened, surely, as he. The old gran turned away in disgust. She would have nothing to do with it. Then the mother, the golden mother beside whom Ben had slept, walked slowly towards the stranger, and Ben realized, by the way she touched him, that she acknowledged him as leader. He would be the father from now on. What if it happened in his own home? What if a neighbour came to fight with his father, and, beating him, drove him away from home? Would his mother mind, would she go to the neighbour?

Ben waited and watched, and then the stranger, who was brown-haired and broad, less graceful than the defeated father, but younger, jerked his head in signal to the mothers to follow him, and meekly, without a word, they obeyed, the children with them. Only the old gran looked backwards across the snow, where, in the distance, stood the smudged figure of the defeated leader, lost and alone.

The battle was over. The day went on as before. As Ben trudged beside his companions through the snow he became accustomed to the new father, the new leader. By afternoon he might have led them always. Perhaps after all he was a relation, an uncle – there was no way of telling what customs they had, the moors.

The sun travelled across the sky and began to sink on the other side of the hills. The company paused once more, and the new father, not so watchful as the first, walked round about the other mother, the aunt – he seemed to like her best. He did not stay on guard as the first father had done. They murmured together, sharing some secret, and when one of the children ran to join them the new father drove him away. He was not going to be so easy of temper as the first.

Ben was faint from hunger now. He went to the mother, the one he knew, the mother of the ragged son, and this time she was patient while he tried to feed, and did not push him away, but suffered him to stay. Ben managed to feed a little, but it was hard. He was not certain of himself, and he was clumsy. After a moment or two the mother moved, and then, as she had done the night before, she settled herself in the snow with her son, and Ben lay down beside her. The others waited around, but Ben had already closed his eyes, his head once more against the shoulder of the mother, his hand in her hair, and whether or not they settled he did not know. Nor did he bother about it, for all that mattered was to be warm and sheltered, protected and cherished by the one he loved.

The angry shouts brought the company to their feet. Bewildered, Ben rubbed his eyes. The moon was full. There, running across the snow, was a crowd of men with sticks, his own father among them, and they were shouting and yelling, waving their sticks at the lordly ones.

This time there was no battle. The leader ran. And with him galloped the mothers, the children, the old gran. They galloped quickly under the moonlight across the frozen snow, and Ben, deserted by his mother, the chestnut mare, deserted by his brothers the moors, the lordly ones, uttered a great cry. He heard the cry tear his chest, and he shouted, "No ... no ... no ..." for the first and the last time, and he fell face downwards in the snow.

The Pool

The Pool

The children ran out on to the lawn. There was space all around them, and light, and air, with the trees indeterminate beyond. The gardener had cut the grass. The lawn was crisp and firm now, because of the hot sun through the day; but near the summer-house where the tall grass stood there were dew-drops like frost clinging to the narrow stems.

The children said nothing. The first moment always took them by surprise. The fact that it waited, thought Deborah, all the time they were away; that day after day while they were at school, or in the Easter holidays with the aunts at Hunstanton being blown to bits, or in the Christmas holidays with their father in London riding on buses and going to theatres – the fact that the garden waited for them was a miracle known only to herself. A year was so long. How did the garden endure the snows clamping down upon it, or the chilly rain that fell in November? Surely sometimes it must mock the slow steps of Grandpapa pacing up and down the terrace in front of the windows, or Grandmama calling to Patch? The garden had to endure month after month of silence, while the children were gone. Even the spring and the days of May and June were wasted, all those mornings of butterflies and darting birds, with no one to watch but Patch gasping for breath on a cool stone slab. So wasted was the garden, so lost.

"You must never think we forget," said Deborah in the silent voice she used to her own possessions. "I remember, even at school, in the middle of French" – but the ache then was unbearable, that it should be the hard grain of a desk under her hands, and not the grass she bent to touch now. The children had had an argument once about whether there was more grass in the world or more sand, and Roger said that of course there must be more sand, because of under the sea; in every ocean all over the world there would be sand, if you looked deep down. But there could be grass too, argued Deborah, a waving grass, a grass that nobody had ever seen, and the colour of that ocean grass would be darker than any grass on the surface of the world, in fields or prairies or people's gardens in America. It would be taller than trees and it would move like corn in a wind.

They had run in to ask somebody adult, "What is there most of in the world, grass or sand?", both children hot and passionate from the argument. But Grandpapa stood there in his old panama hat looking for clippers to trim the hedge – he was rummaging in the drawer full of screws – and he said, "What? What?" impatiently.

The boy turned red – perhaps it was a stupid question – but the girl thought, he doesn't know, they never know, and she made a face at her brother to show that she was on his side. Later they asked their grandmother, and she, being practical, said briskly, "I should think sand. Think of all the grains," and Roger turned in triumph, "I told you so!" The grains. Deborah had not considered the grains. The magic of millions and millions of grains clinging together in the world and under the oceans made her sick. Let Roger win, it did not matter. It was better to be in the minority of the waving grass.

Now, on this first evening of summer holiday, she knelt and then lay full-length on the lawn, and stretched her hands out on either side like Jesus on the Cross, only face downwards, and murmured over and over again the words she had memorized from Confirmation preparation. "A full, perfect and sufficient sacrifice . . . a full, perfect and sufficient sacrifice . . . satisfaction, and oblation, for the sins of the whole world." To offer herself to the earth, to the garden, the garden that had waited patiently all these months since last summer, surely this must be her first gesture.

"Come on," said Roger, rousing himself from his appreciation of how Willis the gardener had mown the lawn to just the right closeness for cricket, and without waiting for his sister's answer he ran to the summer-house and made a dive at the long box in the corner where the stumps were kept. He smiled as he lifted the lid. The familiarity of the smell was satisfying. Old varnish and chipped paint, and surely that must be the same spider and the same cobweb? He drew out the stumps one by one, and the bails, and there was the ball – it had not been lost after all, as he had feared. It was worn, though, a greyish red – he smelt it and bit it, to taste the shabby leather. Then he gathered the things in his arms and went out to set up the stumps.

"Come and help me measure the pitch," he called to his sister, and looking at her, squatting in the grass with her face hidden, his heart sank, because it meant that she was in one of her absent moods and would not concentrate on the cricket.

"Deb?" he called anxiously. "You are going to play?"

Deborah heard his voice through the multitude of earth sounds, the heartbeat and the pulse. If she listened with her ear to the ground there was a humming much deeper than anything that bees did, or the sea at Hunstanton. The nearest to it was the wind, but the wind was reckless. The humming of the earth was patient. Deborah sat up, and her heart sank just as her brother's had done, for the same reason in reverse. The monotony of the game ahead would be like a great chunk torn out of privacy.

"How long shall we have to be?" she called.

The lack of enthusiasm damped the boy. It was not going to be any fun at all if she made a favour of it. He must be firm, though. Any concession on his part she snatched and turned to her advantage.

"Half-an-hour," he said, and then, for encouragement's sake, "You can bat first."

Deborah smelt her knees. They had not yet got the country smell, but if she rubbed them in the grass, and in the earth too, the white London look would go.

"All right," she said, "but no longer than half-an-hour."

He nodded quickly, and so as not to lose time measured out the pitch and then began ramming the stumps in the ground. Deborah went into the summer-house to get the bats. The familiarity of the little wooden hut pleased her as it had her brother. It was a long time now, many years, since they had played in the summer house, making yet another house inside this one with the help of broken deck-chairs; but, just as the garden waited for them a whole year, so did the summer-house, the windows on either side, cobweb-wrapped and stained, gazing out like eyes. Deborah did her ritual of bowing twice. If she should forget this, on her first entrance, it spelt ill-luck.

She picked out the two bats from the corner, where they were stacked with old croquet-hoops, and she knew at once that Roger would choose the one with the rubber handle, even though they could not bat at the same time, and for the whole of the holidays she must make do with the small one, that had half the whipping off. There was a croquet clip lying on the floor. She picked it up and put it on her nose and stood a moment, wondering how it would be if forever more she had to live thus, nostrils pinched, making her voice like Punch. Would people pity her?

"Hurry," shouted Roger, and she threw the clip into the corner, then quickly returned when she was halfway to the pitch, because she knew the clip was lying apart from its fellows, and she might wake in the night and remember it. The clip would turn malevolent, and haunt her. She replaced him on the floor with two others, and now she was absolved and the summer-house at peace.

"Don't get out too soon," warned Roger as she stood in the crease he had marked for her, and with a tremendous effort of concentration Deborah forced her eyes to his retreating figure and watched him roll up his sleeves and pace the required length for his run-up. Down came the ball and she lunged out, smacking it in the air in an easy catch. The impact of ball on bat stung her hands. Roger missed the catch on purpose. Neither of them said anything.

"Who shall I be?" called Deborah.

The game could only be endured, and concentration kept, if Roger gave her a part to play. Not an individual, but a country.

"You're India," he said, and Deborah felt herself grow dark and lean. Part of her was tiger, part of her was sacred cow, the long grass fringing the lawn was jungle, the roof of the summer-house a minaret.

Even so, the half-hour dragged, and, when her turn came to bowl, the ball she threw fell wider every time, so that Roger, flushed and self-conscious because their grandfather had come out on to the terrace and was watching them, called angrily, "Do try."

Once again the effort of concentration, the figure of their grandfather – a source of apprehension to the boy, for he might criticize them – acting as a spur to his sister. Grandpapa was an Indian God, and tribute must be paid to him, a golden apple. The apple must be flung to slay his enemies. Deborah muttered a prayer, and the ball she bowled came fast and true and hit Roger's off-stump. In the moment of delivery their grandfather had turned away and pottered back again through the french windows of the drawing-room.

Roger looked round swiftly. His disgrace had not been seen. "Jolly good ball," he said. "It's your turn to bat again."

But his time was up. The stable clock chimed six. Solemnly Roger drew stumps.

"What shall we do now?" he asked.

Deborah wanted to be alone, but if she said so, on this first evening of the holiday, he would be offended.

"Go to the orchard and see how the apples are coming on," she suggested, "and then round by the kitchen-garden in case the raspberries haven't all been picked. But you have to do it all without meeting anyone. If you see Willis or anyone, even the cat, you lose a mark."

It was these sudden inventions that saved her. She knew her brother would be stimulated at the thought of outwitting the gardener. The aimless wander round the orchard would turn into a stalking exercise.

"Will you come too?" he asked.

"No," she said, "you have to test your skill."

He seemed satisfied with this and ran off towards the orchard, stopping on the way to cut himself a switch from the bamboo.

As soon as he had disappeared Deborah made for the trees fringing the lawn, and once in the shrouded wood felt herself safe. She walked softly along the alley-way to the pool. The late sun sent shafts of light between the trees and on to the alley-way, and a myriad insects webbed their way in the beams, ascending and descending like angels on Jacob's ladder. But were they insects, wondered Deborah, or particles of dust, or even split fragments of light itself, beaten out and scattered by the sun?

It was very quiet. The woods were made for secrecy. They did not recognize her as the garden did. They did not care that for a whole year she could be at school, or at Hunstanton, or in London. The woods would never miss her: they had their own dark, passionate life.

Deborah came to the opening where the pool lay, with the five alley-ways branching from it, and she stood a moment before advancing to the brink, because this was holy ground and required atonement. She crossed her hands on her breast and shut her eyes. Then she kicked off her shoes. "Mother of all things wild, do with me what you will," she said aloud. The sound of her own voice gave her a slight shock. Then she went down on her knees and touched the ground three times with her forehead.

The first part of her atonement was accomplished, but the pool demanded sacrifice, and Deborah had come prepared. There was a stub of pencil she had carried in her pocket throughout the school term which she called her luck. It had teeth marks on it, and a chewed piece of rubber at one end. This treasure must be given to the pool just as other treasures had been given in the past, a miniature jug, a crested button, a china pig. Deborah felt for the stub of pencil and kissed it. She had carried and caressed if for so many lonely months, and now the moment of parting had come. The pool must not be denied. She flung out her right hand, her eyes still shut, and heard the faint plop as the stub of pencil struck the water. Then she opened her eyes, and saw in mid-pool a ripple. The pencil had gone, but the ripple moved, gently shaking the water-lilies. The movement symbolized acceptance.

Deborah, still on her knees and crossing her hands once more, edged her way to the brink of the pool and then, crouching there beside it, looked down into the water. Her reflection wavered up at her, and it was not the face she knew, not even the looking-glass face which anyway was false, but a disturbed image, dark-skinned and ghostly. The crossed hands were like the petals of the water-lilies themselves, and the colour was not waxen white but phantom green. The hair too was not the live clump she brushed every day and tied back with ribbon, but a canopy, a shroud. When the image smiled it became more distorted still. Uncrossing her hands, Deborah leant forward, took a twig, and drew a circle three times on the smooth surface. The water shook in ever widening ripples, and her reflection, broken into fragments, heaved and danced, a sort of monster, and the eyes were there no longer, nor the mouth.

Presently the water became still. Insects, long-legged flies and beetles with spread wings hummed upon it. A dragon-fly had all the magnificence of a lily leaf to himself. He hovered there, rejoicing. But when Deborah took her eyes off him for a moment he was gone. At the far end of the pool, beyond the clustering lilies, green scum had formed, and beneath the scum were rooted, tangled weeds. They were so thick, and had lain in the pool so long, that if a man walked into them from the bank he would be held and choked. A fly, though, or a beetle, could sit upon the surface, and to him the pale green scum would not be treacherous at all, but a resting-place, a haven. And if someone threw a stone, so that the ripples formed, eventually they came to the scum, and rocked it, and the whole of the mossy surface moved in rhythm, a dancing-floor for those who played upon it.

There was a dead tree standing by the far end of the pool. He could have been fir or pine, or even larch, for time had stripped him of identity. He had no distinguishing mark upon his person, but with grotesque limbs straddled the sky. A cap of ivy crowned his raked head. Last winter a dangling branch had broken loose, and this now lay in the pool half-submerged, the green scum dripping from the withered twigs. The soggy branch made a vantage-point for birds, and as Deborah watched a nestling suddenly flew from the undergrowth enveloping the dead tree, and perched for an instant on the mossy filigree. He was lost in terror. The parent bird cried warningly from some dark safety, and the nestling, pricking to the cry, took off from the branch that had offered him temporary salvation. He swerved across the pool, his flight mistimed, yet reached security. The chitter from the undergrowth told of his scolding. When he had gone silence returned to the pool.

It was, so Deborah thought, the time for prayer. The water-lilies were folding upon themselves. The ripples ceased. And that dark hollow in the centre of the pool, that black stillness where the water was deepest, was surely a funnel to the kingdom that lay below. Down that funnel had travelled the discarded treasures. The stub of pencil had lately plunged the depths. He had now been received as an equal among his fellows. This was the single law of the pool, for there were no other commandments. Once it was over, that first cold headlong flight, Deborah knew that the softness of the welcoming water took away all fear. It lapped the face and cleansed the eyes, and the plunge was not into darkness at all but into light. It did not become blacker as the pool was penetrated, but paler, more golden-green, and the mud that people told themselves was there was only a defence against strangers. Those who belonged, who knew, went to the source at once, and there were caverns and fountains and rainbow-coloured seas. There were shores of the whitest sand. There was soundless music.

Once again Deborah closed her eyes and bent lower to the pool. Her lips nearly touched the water. This was the great silence, when she had no thoughts, and was accepted by the pool. Waves of quiet ringed themselves about her, and slowly she lost all feeling, and had no knowledge of her legs, or of her kneeling body, or of her cold, clasped hands. There was nothing but the intensity of peace. It was a deeper acceptance than listening to the earth, because the earth was of the world, the earth was a throbbing pulse, but the acceptance of the pool meant another kind of hearing, a closing in of the waters, and just as the lilies folded so did the soul submerge.

"Deborah . . .? Deborah . . .?" Oh, no! Not now, don't let them call me back now! It was as though someone had hit her on the back, or jumped out at her from behind a corner, the sharp and sudden clamour of another life destroying the silence, the secrecy. And then came the tinkle of the cowbells. It was the signal from their grandmother that the time had come to go in. Not imperious and ugly with authority, like the clanging bell at school summoning those at play to lessons or chapel, but a reminder, nevertheless, that Time was all-important, that life was ruled to order, that even here, in the holiday home the children loved, the adult reigned supreme.

"All right, all right," muttered Deborah, standing up and thrusting her numbed feet into her shoes. This time the rather raised tone of "Deborah?", and the more hurried clanging of the cowbells, brought long ago from Switzerland, suggested a more imperious Grandmama than the tolerant one who seldom questioned. It must mean their supper was already laid, soup perhaps getting cold, and the farce of washing hands, of tidying, of combing hair, must first be gone through.

"Come on, Deb," and now the shout was close, was right at hand, privacy lost forever, for her brother came running down the alley-way swishing his bamboo stick in the air.

"What *have* you been doing?" The question was an intrusion and a threat. She would never have asked him what he had been doing, had he wandered away wanting to be alone, but Roger, alas, did not claim privacy. He liked companionship, and his question now, asked half in irritation, half in resentment, came really from the fear that he might lose her.

"Nothing," said Deborah.

Roger eyed her suspiciously. She was in that morning mood. And it meant, when they went to bed, that she would not talk. One of the best things, in the holidays, was having the two adjoining rooms and calling through to Deb, making her talk.

"Come on," he said, "they've rung," and the making of their grandmother into "they", turning a loved individual into something impersonal, showed Deborah that even if he did not understand he was on her side. He had been called from play, just as she had.

They ran from the woods to the lawn, and on to the terrace. Their grandmother had gone inside, but the cowbells hanging by the french window were still jangling.

The custom was for the children to have their supper first, at seven, and it was laid for them in the dining-room on a hot-plate. They served themselves. At a quarter-to-eight their grandparents had dinner. It was called dinner, but this was a concession to their status. They ate the same as the children, though Grandpapa had a savoury which was not served to the children. If the children were late for supper then it put out Time, as well as Agnes, who cooked for both generations, and it might mean five minutes' delay before Grandpapa had his soup. This shook routine.

The children ran up to the bathroom to wash, then downstairs to the dining-room. Their grandfather was standing in the hall. Deborah sometimes thought that he would have enjoyed sitting with them while they ate their supper, but he never suggested it. Grandmama had warned them, too, never to be a nuisance, or indeed to shout, if Grandpapa was near. This was not because he was nervous, but because he liked to shout himself.

"There's going to be a heat-wave," he said. He had been listening to the news.

"That will mean lunch outside tomorrow," said Roger swiftly. Lunch was the meal they took in common with the grandparents, and it was the moment of the day he disliked. He was nervous that his grandfather would ask him how he was getting on at school.

"Not for me, thank you," said Grandpapa. "Too many wasps."

Roger was at once relieved. This meant that he and Deborah would have the little round garden-table to themselves. But Deborah felt sorry for her grandfather as he went back into the drawing-room. Lunch on the terrace could be gay, and would liven him up. When people grew old they had so few treats.

"What do you look forward to most in the day?" she once asked her grandmother.

"Going to bed," was the reply, "and filling my two hot water bottles." Why work through being young, thought Deborah, to this?

Back in the dining-room the children discussed what they should do during the heat-wave. It would be too hot, Deborah said, for cricket. But they might make a house, suggested Roger, in the trees by the paddock. If he got a few old boards from Willis, and nailed them together like a platform, and borrowed the orchard ladder, then they could take fruit and bottles of orange squash and keep them up there, and it would be a camp from which they could spy on Willis afterwards.

Deborah's first instinct was to say she did not want to play, but she checked herself in time. Finding the boards and fixing them would take Roger a whole morning. It would keep him employed. "Yes, it's a good idea," she said, and to foster his spirit of adventure she looked at his notebook, as they were drinking their soup, and approved of items necessary for the camp while he jotted them down. It was all part of the day-long deceit she practised to express understanding of his way of life.

When they had finished supper they took their trays to the kitchen and watched Agnes, for a moment, as she prepared the second meal for the grandparents. The soup was the same, but garnished. Little croûtons of toasted bread were added to it. And the butter was made into pats, not cut in a slab. The savoury tonight was to be cheese straws. The children finished the ones that Agnes had burnt. Then they went through to the drawing-room to say good night. The older people had both changed. Grandpapa was in a smoking-jacket, and wore soft slippers. Grandmama had a dress that she had worn several years ago in London. She had a cardigan round her shoulders like a cape.

"Go carefully with the bath-water," she said. "We'll be short if there's no rain."

They kissed her smooth, soft skin. It smelt of rose leaves. Grandpapa's chin was sharp and bony. He did not kiss Roger.

"Be quiet overhead," whispered their grandmother. The children nodded. The dining-room was underneath their rooms, and any jumping about or laughter would make a disturbance.

Deborah felt a wave of affection for the two old people. Their lives must be empty and sad. "We *are* glad to be here," she said. Grandmama smiled. This was how she lived, thought Deborah, on little crumbs of comfort.

Once out of the room their spirits soared, and to show relief Roger chased Deborah upstairs, both laughing for no reason. Undressing, they forgot the instructions about the bath, and when they went into the bathroom – Deborah was to have first go – the water was gurgling into the overflow. They tore out the plug in a panic, and listened to the waste roaring down the pipe to the drain below. If Agnes did not have the wireless on she would hear it.

The children were too old now for boats or play, but the bathroom was a place for confidences, for a sharing of those few tastes they agreed upon, or, after quarrelling, for moody silence. The one who broke silence first would then lose face.

"Willis has a new bicycle," said Roger. "I saw it propped against the shed. I couldn't try it because he was there. But I shall tomorrow. It's a Raleigh."

He liked all practical things, and the trying of the gardener's bicycle would give an added interest to the morning of next day.

Willis had a bag of tools in a leather pouch behind the saddle. These could all be felt and the spanners, smelling of oil, tested for shape and usefulness.

"If Willis died," said Deborah, "I wonder what age he would be."

It was the kind of remark that Roger resented always. What had death to do with bicycles? "He's sixty-five," he said, "so he'd be sixty-five."

"No," said Deborah, "what age when he got *there*."

Roger did not want to discuss it. "I bet I can ride it round the stables if I lower the seat," he said. "I bet I don't fall off."

But if Roger would not rise to death, Deborah would not rise to the wager. "Who cares?" she said.

The sudden streak of cruelty stung the brother. Who cared indeed. . . . The horror of an empty world encompassed him, and to give himself confidence he seized the wet sponge and flung it out of the window. They heard it splosh on the terrace below.

"Grandpapa will step on it, and slip," said Deborah, aghast.

The image seized them, and choking back laughter they covered their faces. Hysteria doubled them up. Roger rolled over and over on the bathroom floor. Deborah, the first to recover, wondered why laughter was so near to pain, why Roger's face, twisted now in merriment, was yet the same crumpled thing when his heart was breaking.

"Hurry up," she said briefly, "let's dry the floor," and as they wiped the linoleum with their towels the action sobered them both.

Back in their bedrooms, the door open between them, they watched the light slowly fading. But the air was warm like day. Their grandfather and the people who said what the weather was going to be were right. The heat-wave was on its way. Deborah, leaning out of the open window, fancied she could see it in the sky, a dull haze where the sun had been before; and the trees beyond the lawn, day-coloured when they were having their supper in the dining-room, had turned into night-birds with outstretched wings. The garden knew about the promised heat-wave, and rejoiced: the lack of rain was of no consequence yet, for the warm air was a trap, lulling it into a drowsy contentment.

The dull murmur of their grandparents' voices came from the dining-room below. What did they discuss, wondered Deborah. Did they make those sounds to reassure the children, or were their voices part of their unreal world? Presently the voices ceased, and then there was a scraping of chairs, and voices from a different quarter, the drawing-room now, and a faint smell of their grandfather's cigarette.

Deborah called softly to her brother but he did not answer. She went through to his room, and he was asleep. He must have fallen asleep suddenly, in the midst of talking. She was relieved. Now she could be alone again, and not have to keep up the pretence of sharing conversation. Dusk was everywhere, the sky a deepening black. "When they've gone up to bed," thought Deborah, "then I'll be truly alone." She knew what she was going to do. She waited there, by the open window, and the deepening sky lost the veil that covered it, the haze disintegrated, and the stars broke through. Where there had been nothing was life, dusty and bright, and the waiting earth gave off a scent of knowledge. Dew rose from the pores. The lawn was white.

Patch, the old dog, who slept at the end of Grandpapa's bed on a plaid rug, came out on to the terrace and barked hoarsely. Deborah leant out and threw a piece of creeper on to him. He shook his back. Then he waddled slowly to the flower-tub above the steps and cocked his leg. It was his nightly routine. He barked once more, staring blindly at the hostile trees, and went back into the drawing-room. Soon afterwards, someone came to close the windows – Grandmama, thought Deborah, for the touch was light. "They are shutting out the best," said the child to herself, "all the meaning, and all the point." Patch, being an animal, should know better. He ought to be in a kennel where he could watch, but instead, grown fat and soft, he preferred the bumpiness of her grandfather's bed. He had forgotten the secrets. So had they, the old people.

Deborah heard her grandparents come upstairs. First her grandmother, the quicker of the two, and then her grandfather, more laboured, saying a word or two to Patch as the little dog wheezed his way up. There was a general clicking of lights and shutting of doors. Then silence. How remote, the world of the grandparents, undressing with curtains closed. A pattern of life unchanged for so many years. What went on without would never be known. "He that has ears to hear, let him hear," said Deborah, and she thought of the callousness of Jesus which no priest could explain. Let the dead bury their dead. All the people in the world, undressing now, or sleeping, not just in the village but in cities and capitals, they were shutting out the truth, they were burying their dead. They wasted silence.

The stable clock struck eleven. Deborah pulled on her clothes. Not the cotton frock of the day, but her old jeans that Grandmama disliked, rolled up above her knees. And a jersey. Sandshoes with a hole that did not matter. She was cunning enough to go down by the back stairs. Patch would bark if she tried the front stairs, close to the grandparents' rooms. The back stairs led past Agnes' room, which smelt of apples though she never ate fruit. Deborah could hear her snoring. She would not even wake on Judgement Day. And this led her to wonder on the truth of that fable too, for there might be so many millions by then who liked their graves – Grandpapa, for instance, fond of his routine, and irritated at the sudden riot of trumpets.

Deborah crept past the pantry and the servants' hall – it was only a tiny sitting-room for Agnes, but long usage had given it the dignity of the name – and unlatched and unbolted the heavy back door. Then she stepped outside, on to the gravel, and took the long way round by the front of the house so as not to tread on the terrace, fronting the lawns and the garden.

The warm night claimed her. In a moment it was part of her. She walked on the grass, and her shoes were instantly soaked. She flung up her arms to the sky. Power ran to her fingertips. Excitement was communicated from the waiting trees, and the orchard, and the paddock; the intensity of their secret life caught at her and made her run. It was nothing like the excitement of ordinary looking forward, of birthday presents, of Christmas stockings, but the pull of a magnet – her grandfather had shown her once how it worked, little needles springing to the jaws – and now night and the sky above were a vast magnet, and the things that waited below were needles, caught up in the great demand.

Deborah went to the summer-house, and it was not sleeping like the house fronting the terrace but open to understanding, sharing complicity. Even the dusty windows caught the light, and the cobwebs shone. She rummaged for the old lilo and the moth-eaten car rug that Grandmama had thrown out two summers ago, and bearing them over her shoulder she made her way to the pool. The alley-way was ghostly, and Deborah knew, for all her mounting tension, that the test was hard. Part of her was still body-bound, and afraid of shadows. If anything stirred she would jump and know true terror. She must show defiance, though. The woods expected it. Like old wise lamas they expected courage.

She sensed approval as she ran the gauntlet, the tall trees watching. Any sign of turning back, of panic, and they would crowd upon her in a choking mass, smothering protest. Branches would become arms, gnarled and knotty, ready to strangle, and the leaves of the higher trees fold in and close like the sudden furling of giant umbrellas. The smaller undergrowth, obedient to the will, would become a briary of a million thorns where animals of no known world crouched snarling, their eyes on fire. To show fear was to show misunderstanding. The woods were merciless.

Deborah walked the alley-way to the pool, her left hand holding the lilo and the rug on her shoulder, her right hand raised in salutation. This was a gesture of respect. Then she paused before the pool and laid down her burden beside it. The lilo was to be her bed, the rug her cover. She took off her shoes, also in respect, and lay down upon the lilo. Then, drawing the rug to her chin, she lay flat, her eyes upon the sky. The gauntlet of the alley-way over, she had no more fear. The woods had accepted her, and the pool was the final resting-place, the doorway, the key.

"I shan't sleep," thought Deborah. "I shall just lie awake here all the night and wait for morning, but it will be a kind of introduction to life, like being confirmed."

The stars were thicker now than they had been before. No space in the sky without a prick of light, each star a sun. Some, she thought, were newly born, white-hot, and others wise and colder, nearing completion. The law encompassed them, fixing the riotous path, but how they fell and tumbled depended upon themselves. Such peace, such stillness, such sudden quietude, excitement gone. The trees were no longer menacing but guardians, and the pool was primeval water, the first, the last.

Then Deborah stood at the wicket-gate, the boundary, and there was a woman with outstretched hand, demanding tickets. "Pass through," she said when Deborah reached her. "We saw you coming." The wicket-gate became a turnstile. Deborah pushed against it and there was no resistance, she was through.

"What is it?" she asked. "Am I really here at last? Is this the bottom of the pool?" "It could be," smiled the woman. "There are so many ways. You just happened to choose this one."

Other people were pressing to come through. They had no faces, they were only shadows. Deborah stood aside to let them by, and in a moment they had gone, all phantoms.

"Why only now, tonight?" asked Deborah. "Why not in the afternoon, when I came to the pool?"

"It's a trick," said the woman. "You seize on the moment in time. We were here this afternoon. We're always here. Our life goes on around you, but nobody knows it. The trick's easier by night, that's all."

"Am I dreaming, then?" asked Deborah.

"No," said the woman, "this isn't a dream. And it isn't death, either. It's the secret world."

The secret world. . . . It was something Deborah had always known, and now the pattern was complete. The memory of it, and the relief, were so tremendous that something seemed to burst inside her heart.

"Of course . . ." she said, "of course . . ." and everything that had ever been fell into place. There was no disharmony. The joy was indescribable, and the surge of feeling, like wings about her in the air, lifted her away from the turnstile and the woman, and she had all knowledge. That was it – the invasion of knowledge.

"I'm not myself, then, after all," she thought. "I knew I wasn't. It was only the task given," and, looking down, she saw a little child who was blind trying to find her way. Pity seized her. She bent down and put her hands on the child's eyes, and they opened, and the child was herself at two years old. The incident came back. It was when her mother died and Roger was born.

"It doesn't matter after all," she told the child. "You are not lost. You don't have to go on crying." Then the child that had been herself melted, and became absorbed in the water and the sky, and the joy of the invading flood intensified so that there was no body at all but only being. No words, only movements. And the beating of wings. This above all, the beating of wings.

"Don't let me go!" It was a pulse in her ear, and a cry, and she saw the woman at the turnstile put up her hands to hold her. Then there was such darkness, such dragging, terrible darkness, and the beginning of pain all over again, the leaden heart, the tears, the misunderstanding. The voice saying "No!" was her own harsh, worldly voice, and she was staring at the restless trees, black and ominous against the sky. One hand trailed in the water of the pool.

Deborah sat up, sobbing. The hand that had been in the pool was wet and cold. She dried it on the rug. And suddenly she was seized with such fear that her body took possession, and throwing aside the rug she began to run along the alley-way, the dark trees mocking and the welcome of the woman at the turnstile turned to treachery. Safety lay in the house behind the closed curtains, security was with the grandparents sleeping in their beds, and like a leaf driven before a whirl-wind Deborah was out of the woods and across the silver soaking lawn, up the steps beyond the terrace and through the garden-gate to the back door.

The slumbering solid house received her. It was like an old staid person who, surviving many trials, had learnt experience. "Don't take any notice of them," it seemed to say, jerking its head – did a house have a head? – towards the woods beyond. "They've made no contribution to civilization. I'm man-made and different. This is where you belong, dear child. Now settle down."

Deborah went back again upstairs and into her bedroom. Nothing had changed. It was still the same. Going to the open window she saw that the woods and the lawn seemed unaltered from the moment, how long back she did not know, when she had stood there, deciding upon the visit to the pool. The only difference now was in herself. The excitement had gone, the tension too. Even the terror of those last moments, when her flying feet had brought her to the house, seemed unreal.

She drew the curtains, just as her grandmother might have done, and climbed into bed. Her mind was now preoccupied with practical difficulties, like explaining the presence of the lilo and the rug beside the pool. Willis might find them, and tell her grandfather. The feel of her own pillow, and of her own blankets, reassured her. Both were familiar. And being tired was familiar too, it was a solid bodily ache, like the tiredness after too much jumping or cricket. The thing was, though – and the last remaining conscious thread of thought decided to postpone conclusion until the morning – which was real? This safety of the house, or the secret world?

2

When Deborah woke next morning she knew at once that her mood was bad. It would last her for the day. Her eyes ached, and her neck was stiff, and there was a taste in her mouth like magnesia. Immediately Roger came running into her room, his face refreshed and smiling from some dreamless sleep, and jumped on her bed.

"It's come," he said, "the heat-wave's come. It's going to be ninety in the shade."

Deborah considered how best she could damp his day. "It can go to a hundred for all I care," she said. "I'm going to read all morning."

His face fell. A look of bewilderment came into his eyes. "But the house?" he said. "We'd decided to have a house in the trees, don't you remember?" I was going to get some planks from Willis."

Deborah turned over in bed and humped her knees. "You can, if you like," she said. "I think it's a silly game."

She shut her eyes, feigning sleep, and presently she heard his feet patter slowly back to his own room, and then the thud of a ball against the wall. If he goes on doing that, she thought maliciously, Grandpapa will ring his bell, and Agnes will come panting up the stairs. She hoped for destruction, for grumbling and snapping, and everyone falling out, not speaking. That was the way of the world.

The kitchen, where the children breakfasted, faced west, so it did not get the morning sun. Agnes had hung up fly-papers to catch wasps. The cereal, puffed wheat, was soggy. Deborah complained, mashing the mess with her spoon.

"It's a new packet," said Agnes. "You're mighty particular all of a sudden."

"Deb's got out of bed the wrong side," said Roger.

The two remarks fused to make a challenge. Deborah seized the nearest weapon, a knife, and threw it at her brother. It narrowly missed his eyes, but cut his cheek. Surprised, he put his hand to his face and felt the blood. Hurt, not by the knife but by his sister's action, his face turned red and his lower lip quivered. Deborah ran out of the kitchen and slammed the door. Her own violence distressed her, but the power of the mood was too strong. Going on to the terrace, she saw that the worst had happened. Willis had found the lilo and the rug, and had put them to dry in the sun. He was talking to her grandmother. Deborah tried to slip back into the house, but it was too late.

"Deborah, how very thoughtless of you," said Grandmama. "I tell you children every summer that I don't mind your taking the things from the hut into the garden if only you'll put them back."

Deborah knew she should apologize, but the mood forbade it. "That old rug is full of moth," she said contemptuously, "and the lilo has a rainproof back. It doesn't hurt them."

They both stared at her, and her grandmother flushed, just as Roger had done when she had thrown the knife at him. Then her grandmother turned her back and continued giving some instructions to the gardener.

Deborah stalked along the terrace, pretending that nothing had happened, and skirting the lawn she made her way towards the orchard and so to the fields beyond. She picked up a windfall, but as soon as her teeth bit into it the taste was green. She threw it away. She went and sat on a gate and stared in front of her, looking at nothing. Such deception everywhere. Such sour sadness. It was like Adam and Eve being locked out of paradise. The Garden of Eden was no more. Somewhere, very close, the woman at the turnstile waited to let her in, the secret world was all about her, but the key was gone. Why had she ever come back? What had brought her?

People were going about their business. The old man who came three days a week to help Willis was sharpening his scythe behind the toolshed. Beyond the field where the lane ran towards the main road she could see the top of the postman's head. He was pedalling his bicycle towards the village. She heard Roger calling, "Deb? Deb . . .?", which meant that he had forgiven her, but still the mood held sway and she did not answer. Her own dullness made her own punishment. Presently a knocking sound told her that he had got the planks from Willis and had embarked on the building of his house. He was like his grandfather; he kept to the routine set for himself.

Deborah was consumed with pity. Not for the sullen self humped upon the gate, but for all of them going about their business in the world who did not hold the key. The key was hers, and she had lost it. Perhaps if she worked her way through the long day the magic would return with evening and she would find it once again. Or even now, by the pool, there might be a clue, a vision.

Deborah slid off the gate and went the long way round. By skirting the fields, parched under the sun, she could reach the other side of the wood and meet no one. The husky wheat was stiff. She had to keep close to the hedge to avoid brushing it, and the hedge was tangled. Foxgloves had grown too tall and were bending with empty sockets, their flowers gone. There were nettles everywhere. There was no gate into the wood, and she had to climb the pricking hedge with the barbed wire tearing her knickers. Once in the wood some measure of peace returned, but the alley-ways this side had not been scythed, and the grass was long. She had to wade through it like a sea, brushing it aside with her hands.

She came upon the pool from behind the monster tree, the hybrid whose naked arms were like a dead man's stumps, projecting at all angles. This side, on the lip of the pool, the scum was carpet-thick, and all the lilies, coaxed by the risen sun, had opened wide. They basked as lizards bask on hot stone walls. But here, with stems in water, they swung in grace, cluster upon cluster, pink and waxen white. "They're asleep," thought Deborah. "So is the wood. The morning is not their time," and it seemed to her beyond possibility that the turnstile was at hand and the woman waiting, smiling. "She said they were always there, even in the day, but the truth is that being a child I'm blinded in the day. I don't know how to see."

She dipped her hands in the pool, and the water was tepid brown. She tasted her fingers, and the taste was rank. Brackish water, stagnant from long stillness. Yet beneath . . . beneath, she knew, by night the woman waited, and not only the woman but the whole secret world. Deborah began to pray. "Let it happen again," she whispered. "Let it happen again. Tonight, I won't be afraid."

The sluggish pool made no acknowledgement, but the very silence seemed a testimony of faith, of acceptance. Beside the pool, where the imprint of the lilo had marked the moss, Deborah found a kirby-grip, fallen from her hair during the night. It was proof of visitation. She threw it into the pool as part of the treasury. Then she walked back into the ordinary day and the heat-wave, and her black mood was softened. She went to find Roger in the orchard. He was busy with the platform. Three of the boards were fixed, and the noisy hammering was something that had to be borne. He saw her coming, and as always, after trouble, sensed that her mood had changed and mention must never be made of it. Had he called, "Feeling better?", it would have revived the antagonism, and she might not play with him all the day. Instead, he took no notice. She must be the first to speak.

Deborah waited at the foot of the tree, then bent, and handed him up an apple. It was green, but the offering meant peace. He ate it manfully. "Thanks," he said. She climbed into the tree beside him and reached for the box of nails. Contact had been renewed. All was well between them.

3

The hot day spun itself out like a web. The heat haze stretched across the sky, dun-coloured and opaque. Crouching on the burning boards of the apple-tree, the children drank gingerbeer and fanned themselves with dock-leaves. They grew hotter still. When the cowbells summoned them for lunch they found that their grandmother had drawn the curtains of all the rooms downstairs, and the drawing-room was a vault and strangely cool. They flung themselves into chairs. No one was hungry. Patch lay under the piano, his soft mouth dripping saliva. Grandmama had changed into a sleeveless linen dress never before seen, and Grandpapa, in a dented panama, carried a fly-whisk used years ago in Egypt.

"Ninety-one," he said grimly, "on the Air Ministry roof. It was on the one o'clock news."

Deborah thought of the men who must measure heat, toiling up and down on this Ministry roof with rods and tapes and odd-shaped instruments. Did anyone care but Grandpapa?

"Can we take our lunch outside?" asked Roger.

His grandmother nodded. Speech was too much effort, and she sank languidly into her chair at the foot of the dining-room table. The roses she had picked last night had wilted.

The children carried chicken drumsticks to the summer-house. It was too hot to sit inside, but they sprawled in the shadow it cast, their heads on faded cushions shedding kapok. Somewhere, far above their heads, an aeroplane climbed like a small silver fish, and was lost in space.

"A Meteor," said Roger. "Grandpapa says they're obsolete."

Deborah thought of Icarus, soaring towards the sun. Did he know when his wings began to melt? How did he feel? She stretched out her arms and thought of them as wings. The fingertips would be the first to curl, and then turn cloggy soft, and useless. What terror in the sudden loss of height, the drooping power . . .

Roger, watching her, hoped it was some game. He threw his picked drumstick into a flower-bed and jumped to his feet.

"Look," he said, "I'm a Javelin," and he too stretched his arms and ran in circles, banking. Jet noises came from his clenched teeth. Deborah dropped her arms and looked at the drumstick. What had been clean and white from Roger's teeth was now earth-brown. Was it offended to be chucked away? Years later, when everyone was dead, it would be found, moulded like a fossil. Nobody would care.

"Come on," said Roger.

"Where to?" she asked.

"To fetch the raspberries," he said.

"You go," she told him.

Roger did not like going into the dining-room alone. He was

self-conscious. Deborah made a shield from the adult eyes. In the end he consented to fetch the raspberries without her on condition that she played cricket after tea. After tea was a long way off.

She watch him return, walking very slowly, bearing the plates of raspberries and clotted cream. She was seized with sudden pity, that same pity which, earlier, she had felt for all people other than herself. How absorbed he was, how intent on the moment that held him. But tomorrow he would be some old man far away, the garden forgotten, and this day long past.

"Grandmama says it can't go on," he announced. "There'll have to be a storm."

But why? Why not forever? Why not breathe a spell so that all of them could stay locked and dreaming like the courtiers in the *Sleeping Beauty*, never knowing, never waking, cobwebs in their hair and on their hands, tendrils imprisoning the house itself?

"Race me," said Roger, and to please him she plunged her spoon into the mush of raspberries but finished last, to his delight.

No one moved during the long afternoon. Grandmama went upstairs to her room. The children saw her at her window in her petticoat drawing the curtains close. Grandpapa put his feet up in the drawing-room, a handkerchief over his face. Patch did not stir from his place under the piano. Roger, undefeated, found employment still. He first helped Agnes to shell peas for supper, squatting on the back-door step while she relaxed on a lop-sided basket chair dragged from the servants' hall. This task finished, he discovered a tin-bath, put away in the cellar, in which Patch had been washed in younger days. He carried it to the lawn and filled it with water. Then he stripped to bathing-trunks and sat in it solemnly, an umbrella over his head to keep off the sun.

Deborah lay on her back behind the summer-house, wondering what would happen if Jesus and Buddha met. Would there be discussion, courtesy, an exchange of views like politicians at summit talks? Or were they after all the same person, born at separate times? The queer thing was that this topic, interesting now, meant nothing in the secret world. Last night, through the turnstile, all problems disappeared. They were non-existent. There was only the knowledge and the joy.

She must have slept, because when she opened her eyes she saw to her dismay that Roger was no longer in the bath but was hammering the cricket-stumps into the lawn. It was a quarter-to-five.

"Hurry up," he called, when he saw her move. "I've had tea."

She got up and dragged herself into the house, sleepy still, and giddy. The grandparents were in the drawing-room, refreshed from the long repose of the afternoon. Grandpapa smelt of eau-de-cologne. Even Patch had come to and was lapping his saucer of cold tea.

"You look tired," said Grandmama critically. "Are you feeling all right?"

Deborah was not sure. Her head was heavy. It must have been sleeping in the afternoon, a thing she never did.

"I think so," she answered, "but if anyone gave me roast pork I know I'd be sick."

"No one suggested you should eat roast pork," said her grandmother, surprised. "Have a cucumber sandwich, they're cool enough."

Grandpapa was lying in wait for a wasp. He watched it hover over his tea, grim, expectant. Suddenly he slammed at the air with his whisk. "Got the brute," he said in triumph. He ground it into the carpet with his heel. It made Deborah think of Jehovah.

"Don't rush around in the heat," said Grandmama. "It isn't wise. Can't you and Roger play some nice, quiet game?"

"What sort of game?" asked Deborah.

But her grandmother was without invention. The croquet mallets were all broken. "We might pretend to be dwarfs and use the heads," said Deborah, and she toyed for a moment with the idea of squatting to croquet. Their knees would stiffen, though, it would be too difficult.

"I'll read aloud to you, if you like," said Grandmama.

Deborah seized upon the suggestion. It delayed cricket. She ran out on to the lawn and padded the idea to make it acceptable to Roger.

"I'll play afterwards," she said, "and that ice-cream that Agnes has in the fridge, you can eat all of it. I'll talk tonight in bed."

Roger hesitated. Everything must be weighed. Three goods to balance evil.

"You know that stick of sealing-wax Daddy gave you?" he said.

"Yes."

"Can I have it?"

The balance for Deborah too. The quiet of the moment in opposition to the loss of the long thick stick so brightly red.

"All right," she grudged.

Roger left the cricket stumps and they went into the drawing-room. Grandpapa, at the first suggestion of reading aloud, had disappeared, taking Patch with him. Grandmama had cleared away the tea. She found her spectacles and the book. It was *Black Beauty*. Grandmama kept no modern children's books, and this made common ground for the three of them. She read the terrible chapter where the stable-lad lets Beauty get overheated and gives him a cold drink and does not put on his blanket. The story was suited to the day. Even Roger listened entranced. And Deborah, watching her grandmother's calm face and hearing her careful voice reading the sentences, thought how strange it was that Grandmama could turn herself into Beauty with such ease. She *was* a horse, suffering there with pneumonia in the stable, being saved by the wise coachman.

After the reading, cricket was anti-climax, but Deborah must keep her bargain. She kept thinking of Black Beauty writing the book. It showed how good the story was, Grandmama said, because no child had ever yet questioned the practical side of it, or posed the picture of a horse with a pen in its hoof.

"A modern horse would have a typewriter," thought Deborah, and she began to bowl to Roger, smiling to herself as she did so because of the twentieth-century Beauty clacking with both hoofs at a machine.

This evening, because of the heat-wave, the routine was changed. They had their baths first, before their supper, for they were hot and exhausted from the cricket. Then, putting on pyjamas and cardigans, they ate their supper on the terrace. For once Grandmama was indulgent. It was still so hot that they could not take chill, and the dew had not yet risen. It made a small excitement, being in pyjamas on the terrace. Like people abroad, said Roger. Or natives in the South Seas, said Deborah. Or beachcombers who had lost caste. Grandpapa, changed into a white tropical jacket, had not lost caste.

"He's a white trader," whispered Deborah. "He's made a fortune out of pearls."

Roger choked. Any joke about his grandfather, whom he feared, had all the sweet agony of danger.

"What's the thermometer say?" asked Deborah.

Her grandfather, pleased at her interest, went to inspect it.

"Still above eighty," he said with relish.

Deborah, when she cleaned her teeth later, thought how pale her face looked in the mirror above the wash-basin. It was not brown, like Roger's, from the day in the sun, but wan and yellow. She tied back her hair with a ribbon, and the nose and chin were peaky sharp. She yawned largely, as Agnes did in the kitchen on Sunday afternoons.

"Don't forget you promised to talk," said Roger quickly.

Talk. . . . That was the burden. She was so tired she longed for the white smoothness of her pillow, all blankets thrown aside, bearing only a single sheet. But Roger, wakeful on his bed, the door between them wide, would not relent. Laughter was the one solution, and to make him hysterical, and so exhaust him sooner, she fabricated a day in the life of Willis, from his first morning kipper to his final glass of beer at the village inn. The adventures in between would have tried Gulliver. Roger's delight drew protests from the adult world below. There was the sound of a bell, and then Agnes came up the stairs and put her head round the corner of Deborah's door.

"Your Granny says you're not to make so much noise," she said.

Deborah, spent with invention, lay back and closed her eyes. She could go no further. The children called good night to each other, both speaking at the same time, from age-long custom, beginning with their names and addresses and ending with the world, the universe, and space. Then the final main "Good night," after which neither must ever speak, on pain of unknown calamity.

"I must try and keep awake," thought Deborah, but the power was not in her. Sleep was too compelling, and it was hours later that she opened her eyes and saw her curtains blowing and the forked flash light the ceiling, and heard the trees tossing and sobbing against the sky. She was out of bed in an instant. Chaos had come. There were no stars, and the night was sulphurous. A great crack split the heavens and tore them in two. The garden groaned. If the rain would only fall there might be mercy, and the trees, imploring, bowed themselves this way and that, while the vivid lawn, bright in expectation, lay like a sheet of metal exposed to flame. Let the waters break. Bring down the rain.

Suddenly the lightning forked again, and standing there, alive yet immobile, was the woman by the turnstile. She stared up at the windows of the house, and Deborah recognized her. The turnstile was there, inviting entry, and already the phantom figures, passing through it, crowded towards the trees beyond the lawn. The secret world was waiting. Through the long day, while the storm was brewing, it had hovered there unseen beyond her reach, but now that night had come, and the thunder with it, the barriers were down. Another crack, mighty in its summons, the turnstile yawned, and the woman with her hand upon it smiled and beckoned.

Deborah ran out of the room and down the stairs. Somewhere somebody called – Roger, perhaps, it did not matter – and Patch was barking; but caring nothing for concealment she went through the dark drawing-room and opened the french window on to the terrace. The lightning searched the terrace and lit the paving, and Deborah ran down the steps on to the lawn where the turnstile gleamed.

Haste was imperative. If she did not run the turnstile might be closed, the woman vanish, and all the wonder of the sacred world be taken from her. She was in time. The woman was still waiting. She held out her hand for tickets, but Deborah shook her head. "I have none." The woman, laughing, brushed her through into the secret world where there were no laws, no rules, and all the faceless phantoms ran before her to the woods, blown by the rising wind. Then the rain came. The sky, deep brown as the lightning pierced it, opened, and the water hissed to the ground, rebounding from the earth in bubbles. There was no order now in the alley-way. The ferns had turned to trees, the trees to Titans. All moved in ecstasy, with sweeping limbs, but the rhythm was broken up, tumultuous, so that some of them were bent backwards, torn by the sky, and others dashed their heads to the undergrowth where they were caught and beaten.

In the world behind, laughed Deborah as she ran, this would be punishment, but here in the secret world it was a tribute. The phantoms who ran beside her were like waves. They were linked one with another, and they were, each one of them, and Deborah too, part of the night force that made the sobbing and the laughter. The lightning forked where they willed it, and the thunder cracked as they looked upwards to the sky.

The pool had come alive. The water-lilies had turned to hands, with palms upraised, and in the far corner, usually so still under the green scum, bubbles sucked at the surface, steaming and multiplying as the torrents fell. Everyone crowded to the pool. The phantoms bowed and crouched by the water's edge, and now the woman had set up her turnstile in the middle of the pool, beckoning them once more. Some remnant of a sense of social order rose in Deborah and protested.

"But we've already paid," she shouted, and remembered a second later that she had passed through free. Must there be duplication? Was the secret world a rainbow, always repeating itself, alighting on another hill when you believed yourself beneath it? No time to think. The phantoms had gone through. The lightning, streaky white, lit the old dead monster tree with his crown of ivy, and because he had no spring now in his joints he could not sway in tribute with the trees and ferns, but had to remain there, rigid, like a crucifix.

"And now . . . and now . . . and now . . ." called Deborah.

The triumph was that she was not afraid, was filled with such wild acceptance. . . . She ran into the pool. Her living feet felt the mud and the broken sticks and all the tangle of old weeds, and the water was up to her armpits and her chin. The lilies held her. The rain blinded her. The woman and the turnstile were no more.

"Take me too," cried the child. "Don't leave me behind!" In her heart was a savage disenchantment. They had broken their promise, they had left her in the world. The pool that claimed her now was not the pool of secrecy, but dank, dark, brackish water choked with scum.

4

"Grandpapa says he's going to have it fenced round," said Roger. "It should have been done years ago. A proper fence, then nothing can ever happen. But barrow-loads of shingle tipped in it first. Then it won't be a pool, but just a dewpond. Dewponds aren't dangerous."

He was looking at her over the edge of her bed. He had risen in status, being the only one of them downstairs, the bearer of tidings good or ill, the go-between. Deborah had been ordered two days in bed.

"I should think by Wednesday," he went on, "you'd be able to play cricket. It's not as if you're hurt. People who walk in their sleep are just a bit potty."

"I did not walk in my sleep," said Deborah.

"Grandpapa said you must have done," said Roger. "It was a good thing that Patch woke him up and he saw you going across the lawn . . ." Then, to show his release from tension, he stood on his hands.

Deborah could see the sky from her bed. It was flat and dull. The day was a summer day that had worked through storm. Agnes came into the room with junket on a tray. She looked important.

"Now run off," she said to Roger. "Deborah doesn't want to

talk to you. She's supposed to rest."

Surprisingly, Roger obeyed, and Agnes placed the junket on the table beside the bed. "You don't feel hungry, I expect," she said. "Never mind, you can eat this later, when you fancy it. Have you got a pain? It's usual, the first time."

"No," said Deborah.

What had happened to her was personal. They had prepared her for it at school, but nevertheless it was a shock, not to be discussed with Agnes. The woman hovered a moment, in case the child asked questions; but, seeing that none came, she turned and left the room.

Deborah, her cheek on her hand, stared at the empty sky. The heaviness of knowledge lay upon her, a strange, deep sorrow.

"I won't come back," she thought, "I've lost the key."

The hidden world, like ripples on the pool so soon to be filled in and fenced, was out of her reach for ever.

The Old Man

The Old Man

Did I hear you asking about the Old Man? I thought so. You're a newcomer to the district, here on holiday. We get plenty these days, during the summer months. Somehow they always find their way eventually over the cliffs down to this beach, and then they pause and look from the sea back to the lake. Just as you did.

It's a lovely spot, isn't it? Quiet and remote. You can't wonder at the old man choosing to live here.

I don't remember when he first came. Nobody can. Many years ago, it must have been. He was here when I arrived, long before the war. Perhaps he came to escape from civilization, much as I did myself. Or maybe, where he lived before, the folks around made things too hot for him. It's hard to say. I had the feeling, from the very first, that he had done something, or something had been done to him, that gave him a grudge against the world. I remember the first time I set eyes on him I said to myself, "I bet that old fellow is one hell of a character."

Yes, he was living here beside the lake, along of his missus. Funny sort of lash-up they had, exposed to all the weather, but they didn't seem to mind.

I had been warned about him by one of the fellows from the farm, who advised me, with a grin, to give the old man who lived down by the lake a wide berth – he didn't care for strangers. So I went warily, and I didn't stay to pass the time of day. Nor would it have been any use if I had, not knowing a word of his lingo. The first time I saw him he was standing by the edge of the lake, looking out to sea, and from tact I avoided the piece of planking over the stream, which meant passing close to him, and crossed to the other side of the lake by the beach instead. Then, with an awkward feeling that I was trespassing and had no business to be there, I bobbed down behind a clump of gorse, took out my spy-glass, and had a peep at him.

He was a big fellow, broad and strong – he's aged, of course, lately; I'm speaking of several years back – but even now you can see what he must have been once. Such power and drive behind him, and that fine head, which he carried like a king. There's an idea in that, too. No, I'm not joking. Who knows what royal blood he carries inside him, harking back to some remote ancestor? And now and again, surging in him – not through his own fault – it gets the better of him and drives him fighting mad. I didn't think about that at the time. I just looked at him, and ducked behind the gorse when I saw him turn, and I wondered to myself what went on in his mind, whether he knew I was there, watching him.

If he should decide to come up the lake after me I should look pretty foolish. He must have thought better of it, though, or perhaps he did not care. He went on staring out to sea, watching the gulls and the incoming tide, and presently he ambled off his side of the lake, heading for the missus and home and maybe supper.

I didn't catch a glimpse of her that first day. She just wasn't around. Living as they do, close in by the left bank of the lake, with no proper track to the place, I hardly had the nerve to venture close and come upon her face to face. When I did see her, though, I was disappointed. She wasn't much to look at after all. What I mean is, she hadn't got anything like his character. A placid, mild-tempered creature, I judged her.

They had both come back from fishing when I saw them, and were making their way up from the beach to the lake. He was in front, of course. She tagged along behind. Neither of them took the slightest notice of me, and I was glad, because the old man might have paused, and waited, and told her to get on back home, and then come down towards the rocks where I was sitting. You ask what I would have said, had he done so? I'm damned if I know. Maybe I would have got up, whistling and seeming unconcerned, and then, with a nod and a smile – useless, really, but instinctive, if you know what I mean – said good day and pottered off. I don't think he would have done anything. He'd just have stared after me, with those strange narrow eyes of his, and let me go.

After that, winter and summer, I was always down on the beach or the rocks, and they went on living their curious, remote existence, sometimes fishing in the lake, sometimes at sea. Occasionally I'd come across them in the harbour on the estuary, taking a look at the yachts anchored there, and the shipping. I used to wonder which of them made the suggestion. Perhaps suddenly he would be lured by the thought of the bustle and life of the harbour, and all the things he had either wantonly given up or never known, and he would say to her, "Today we are going into town." And she, happy to do whatever pleased him best, followed along.

You see, one thing that stood out – and you couldn't help noticing it – was that the pair of them were devoted to one another. I've seen her greet him when he came back from a day's fishing and had left her back home, and towards evening she'd come down the lake and on to the beach and down to the sea to wait for him. She'd see him coming from a long way off, and I would see him too, rounding the corner of the bay. He'd come straight in to the beach, and she would go to meet him, and they would embrace each other, not caring a damn who saw them. It was touching, if you know what I mean. You felt there was something lovable about the old man, if that's how things were between them. He might be a devil to outsiders, but he was all the world to her. It gave me a warm feeling for him, when I saw them together like that.

You asked if they had any family? I was coming to that. It's about the family I really wanted to tell you. Because there was a tragedy, you see. And nobody knows anything about it except me. I suppose I could have told someone, but if I had, I don't know . . . They might have taken the old man away, and she'd have broken her heart without him, and anyway, when all's said and done, it wasn't my business. I know the evidence against the old man was strong, but I hadn't positive proof, it might have been some sort of accident, and anyway, nobody made any inquiries at the time the boy disappeared, so who was I to turn busybody and informer?

I'll try and explain what happened. But you must understand that all this took place over quite a time, and sometimes I was away from home or busy, and didn't go near the lake. Nobody seemed to take any interest in the couple living there but myself, so that it was only what I observed with my own eyes that makes this story, nothing that I heard from anybody else, no scraps of gossip, or tales told about them behind their backs.

Yes, they weren't always alone, as they are now. They had four kids. Three girls and a boy. They brought up the four of them in that ramshackle old place by the lake, and it was always a wonder to me how they did it. God, I've known days when the rain lashed the lake into little waves that burst and broke on the muddy shore near by their place, and turned the marsh into a swamp, and the wind driving straight in. You'd have thought anyone with a grain of sense would have taken his missus and his kids out of it and gone off somewhere where they could get some creature comforts at least. Not the old man. If he could stick it, I guess he decided she could too, and the kids as well. Maybe he wanted to bring them up the hard way.

Mark you, they were attractive youngsters. Especially the youngest girl. I never knew her name, but I called her Tiny, she had so much go to her. Chip off the old block, in spite of her size. I can see her now, as a little thing, the first to venture paddling in the lake, on a fine morning, way ahead of her sisters and the brother.

The brother I nicknamed Boy. He was the eldest, and between you and me a bit of a fool. He hadn't the looks of his sisters and was a clumsy sort of fellow. The girls would play around on their own, and go fishing, and he'd hang about in the background, not knowing what to do with himself. If he possibly could he'd stay around home, near his mother. Proper mother's boy. That's why I gave him the name. Not that she seemed to fuss over him any more than she did the others. She treated the four alike, as far as I could tell. Her thoughts were always for the old man rather than for them. But Boy was just a great baby, and I have an idea he was simple.

Like the parents, the youngsters kept themselves to themselves. Been dinned into them, I dare say, by the old man. They never came down to the beach on their own and played; and it must have been a temptation, I thought, in full summer, when people came walking over the cliffs down to the beach to bathe and picnic. I suppose, for those strange reasons best known to himself, the old man had warned them to have no truck with strangers.

They were used to me pottering, day in, day out, fetching driftwood and that. And often I would pause and watch the kids playing by the lake. I didn't talk to them, though. They might have gone back and told the old man. They used to look up when I passed by, then glance away again, sort of shy. All but Tiny. Tiny would toss her head and do a somersault, just to show off.

I sometimes watched them go off, the six of them – the old man, the missus, Boy, and the three girls, for a day's fishing out to sea. The old man, of course, in charge; Tiny eager to help, close to her dad; the missus looking about her to see if the weather was going to keep fine; the two other girls alongside; and Boy, poor simple Boy, always the last to leave home. I never knew what sport they had. They used to stay out late, and I'd have left the beach by the time they came back again. But I guess they did well. They must have lived almost entirely on what they caught. Well, fish is said to be full of vitamins, isn't it? Perhaps the old man was a food faddist in his way.

Time passed, and the youngsters began to grow up. Tiny lost something of her individuality then, it seemed to me. She grew more like her sisters. They were a nice-looking trio, all the same. Quiet, you know, well-behaved.

As for Boy, he was enormous. Almost as big as the old man, but with what a difference! He had none of his father's looks, or strength, or personality; he was nothing but a great clumsy lout. And the trouble was, I believe the old man was ashamed of him. He didn't pull his weight in the home, I'm certain of that. And out fishing he was perfectly useless. The girls would work away like beetles, with Boy, always in the background, making a mess of things. If his mother was there he just stayed by her side.

I could see it rattled the old man to have such an oaf of a son. Irritated him, too, because Boy was so big. It probably didn't make sense to his intolerant mind. Strength and stupidity didn't go together. In any normal family, of course, Boy would have left home by now and gone out to work. I used to wonder if they argued about it back in the evenings, the missus and the old man, or if it was something never admitted between them but tacitly understood – Boy was no good.

Well, they did leave home at last. At least, the girls did.

I'll tell you how it happened.

It was a day in late autumn, and I happened to be over doing some shopping in the little town overlooking the harbour, three miles from this place, and suddenly I saw the old man, the missus, the three girls and Boy all making their way up to Pont – that's at the head of a creek going eastward from the harbour. There are a few cottages at Pont, and a farm and a church up behind. The family looked washed and spruced up, and so did the old man and the missus, and I wondered if they were going visiting. If they were, it was an unusual thing for them to do. But it's possible they had friends or acquaintances up there, of whom I knew nothing. Anyway, that was the last I saw of them, on the fine Saturday afternoon, making for Pont.

It blew hard over the week-end, a proper easterly gale. I kept indoors and didn't go out at all. I knew the seas would be breaking good and hard on the beach. I wondered if the old man and the family had been able to get back. They would have been wise to stay with their friends up Pont, if they had friends there.

It was Tuesday before the wind dropped and I went down to the beach again. Seaweed, driftwood, tar and oil all over the place. It's always the same after an easterly blow. I looked up the lake, towards the old man's shack, and I saw him there, with the missus, just by the edge of the lake. But there was no sign of the youngsters.

I thought it a bit funny, and waited around in case they should appear. They never did. I walked right round the lake, and from the opposite bank I had a good view of their place, and even took out my old spy-glass to have a closer look. They just weren't there. The old man was pottering about as he often did when he wasn't fishing, and the missus had settled herself down to bask in the sun. There was only one explanation. They had left the family with friends in Pont. They had sent the family for a holiday.

I can't help admitting I was relieved, because for one frightful moment I thought maybe they had started off back home on the Saturday night and got struck by the gale; and, well – that the old man and his missus had got back safely, but not the kids. It couldn't be that, though. I should have heard. Someone would have said something. The old man wouldn't be pottering there in his usual unconcerned fashion and the missus basking in the sun. No, that must have been it. They had left the family with friends. Or maybe the girls and Boy had gone up country, gone to find themselves jobs at last.

Somehow it left a gap. I felt sad. So long now I had been used to seeing them all around, Tiny and the others. I had a strange sort of feeling that they had gone for good. Silly, wasn't it? To mind, I mean. There was the old man, and his missus, and the four youngsters, and I'd more or less watched them grow up, and now for no reason they had gone.

I wished then I knew even a word or two of his language, so that I could have called out to him, neighbour-like, and said, "I see you and the missus are on your own. Nothing wrong, I hope?"

But there, it wasn't any use. He'd have looked at me with his strange eyes and told me to go to hell.

I never saw the girls again. No, never. They just didn't come back. Once I thought I saw Tiny, somewhere up the estuary, with a group of friends, but I couldn't be sure. If it was, she'd grown, she looked different. I tell you what I think. I think the old man and the missus took them with a definite end in view, that last week-end, and either settled them with friends they knew or told them to shift for themselves.

I know it sounds hard, not what you'd do for your own son and daughters, but you have to remember the old man was a tough customer, a law unto himself. No doubt he thought it would be for the best, and so it probably was, and if only I could know for certain what happened to the girls, especially Tiny, I wouldn't worry.

But I do worry sometimes, because of what happened to Boy.

You see, Boy was fool enough to come back. He came back about three weeks after that final week-end. I had walked down through the woods – not my usual way, but down to the lake by the stream that feeds it from a higher level. I rounded the lake by the marshes to the north, some distance from the old man's place, and the first thing I saw was Boy.

He wasn't doing anything. He was just standing by the marsh. He looked dazed. He was too far off for me to hail him; besides, I didn't have the nerve. But I watched him, as he stood there in his clumsy loutish way, and I saw him staring at the far end of the lake. He was staring in the direction of the old man.

The old man, and the missus with him, took not the slightest notice of Boy. They were close to the beach, by the plank bridge, and were either just going out to fish or coming back. And here was Boy, with his dazed stupid face, but not only stupid – frightened.

I wanted to say, "Is anything the matter?" but I didn't know how to say it. I stood there, like Boy, staring at the old man.

Then what we both must have feared would happen, happened.

The old man lifted his head, and saw Boy.

He must have said a word to his missus, because she didn't move, she stayed where she was, by the bridge, but the old man turned like a flash of lightning and came down the other side of the lake towards the marshes, towards Boy. He looked terrible. I shall never forget his appearance. That magnificent head I had always admired now angry, evil; and he was cursing Boy as he came. I tell you, I heard him.

Boy, bewildered, scared, looked hopelessly about him for cover. There was none. Only the thin reeds that grew beside the marsh. But the poor fellow was so dumb he went in there, and crouched, and believed himself safe – it was a horrible sight.

I was just getting my own courage up to interfere when the old man stopped suddenly in his tracks, pulled up short as it were, and then, still cursing, muttering, turned back again and returned to the bridge. Boy watched him, from his cover of reeds, then, poor clot that he was, came out on to the marsh again, with some idea, I suppose, of striking for home.

I looked about me. There was no one to call. No one to give any help. And if I went and tried to get someone from the farm they would tell me not to interfere, that the old man was best left alone when he got in one of his rages, and anyway that Boy was old enough to take care of himself. He was as big as the old man. He could give as good as he got. I knew different. Boy was no fighter. He didn't know how.

I waited quite a time beside the lake but nothing happened. It began to grow dark. It was no use my waiting there. The old man and the missus left the bridge and went on home. Boy was still standing there on the marsh, by the lake's edge.

I called to him, softly. "It's no use. He won't let you in. Go back to Pont, or wherever it is you've been. Go to some place, anywhere, but get out of here."

He looked up, that same queer dazed expression on his face, and I could tell he hadn't understood a word I said.

I felt powerless to do any more. I went home myself. But I thought about Boy all evening, and in the morning I went down to the lake again, and I took a great stick with me to give me courage. Not that it would have been much good. Not against the old man.

Well . . . I suppose they had come to some sort of agreement, during the night. There was Boy, by his mother's side, and the old man was pottering on his own.

I must say, it was a great relief. Because, after all, what could I have said or done? If the old man didn't want Boy home, it was really his affair. And if Boy was too stupid to go, that was Boy's affair.

But I blamed the mother a good deal. After all, it was up to her to tell Boy he was in the way, and the old man was in one of his moods, and Boy had best get out while the going was good. But I never did think she had great intelligence. She did not seem to show much spirit at any time.

However, what arrangement they had come to worked for a time. Boy stuck close to his mother – I suppose he helped her at home, I don't know – and the old man left them alone and was more and more by himself.

He took to sitting down by the bridge, humped, staring out to sea, with a queer brooding look on him. He seemed strange, and lonely. I didn't like it. I don't know what his thoughts were, but I'm sure they were evil. It suddenly seemed a very long time since he and the missus and the whole family had gone fishing, a happy, contented party. Now everything had changed for him. He was thrust out in the cold, and the missus and Boy stayed together.

I felt sorry for him, but I felt frightened too. Because I felt it could not go on like this indefinitely; something would happen.

One day I went down to the beach for driftwood – it had been blowing in the night – and when I glanced towards the lake I saw that Boy wasn't with his mother. He was back where I had seen him that first day, on the edge of the marsh. He was as big as his father. If he'd known how to use his strength he'd have been a match for him any day, but he hadn't the brains. There he was, back on the marsh, a great big frightened foolish fellow, and there was the old man, outside his home, staring down towards his son with murder in his eyes.

I said to myself, "He's going to kill him." But I didn't know how or when or where, whether by night, when they were sleeping, or by day, when they were fishing. The mother was useless, she would not prevent it. It was no use appealing to the mother. If only Boy would use one little grain of sense, and go . . .

I watched and waited until nightfall. Nothing happened.

It rained in the night. It was grey, and cold, and dim. December was everywhere, trees all bare and bleak. I couldn't get down to the lake until late afternoon, and then the skies had cleared and the sun was shining in that watery way it does in winter, a burst of it, just before setting below the sea.

I saw the old man, and the missus too. They were close together, by the old shack, and they saw me coming for they looked towards me. Boy wasn't there. He wasn't on the marsh, either. Nor by the side of the lake.

I crossed the bridge and went along the right bank of the lake, and I had my spy-glass with me, but I couldn't see Boy. Yet all the time I was aware of the old man watching me.

Then I saw him. I scrambled down the bank, and crossed the marsh, and went to the thing I saw lying there, behind the reeds.

He was dead. There was a great gash on his body. Dried blood on his back. But he had lain there all night. His body was sodden with the rain.

Maybe you'll think I'm a fool, but I began to cry, like an idiot, and I shouted across to the old man, "You murderer, you bloody God-damned murderer." He did not answer. He did not move. He stood there, outside his shack with the missus, watching me.

You'll want to know what I did. I went back and got a spade, and I dug a grave for Boy, in the reeds behind the marsh, and I said one of my own prayers for him, being uncertain of his religion. When I had finished I looked across the lake to the old man.

And do you know what I saw?

I saw him lower his great head, and bend towards her and embrace her. And she lifted her head to him and embraced him too. It was both a requiem and a benediction. An atonement, and a giving of praise. In their strange way they knew they had done evil, but now it was over, because I had buried Boy and he was gone. They were free to be together again, and there was no longer a third to divide them.

They came out into the middle of the lake, and suddenly I saw the old man stretch his neck and beat his wings, and he took off from the water, full of power, and she followed him. I watched the two swans fly out to sea right into the face of the setting sun, and I tell you it was one of the most beautiful sights I ever saw in my life: the two swans flying there, alone, in winter.

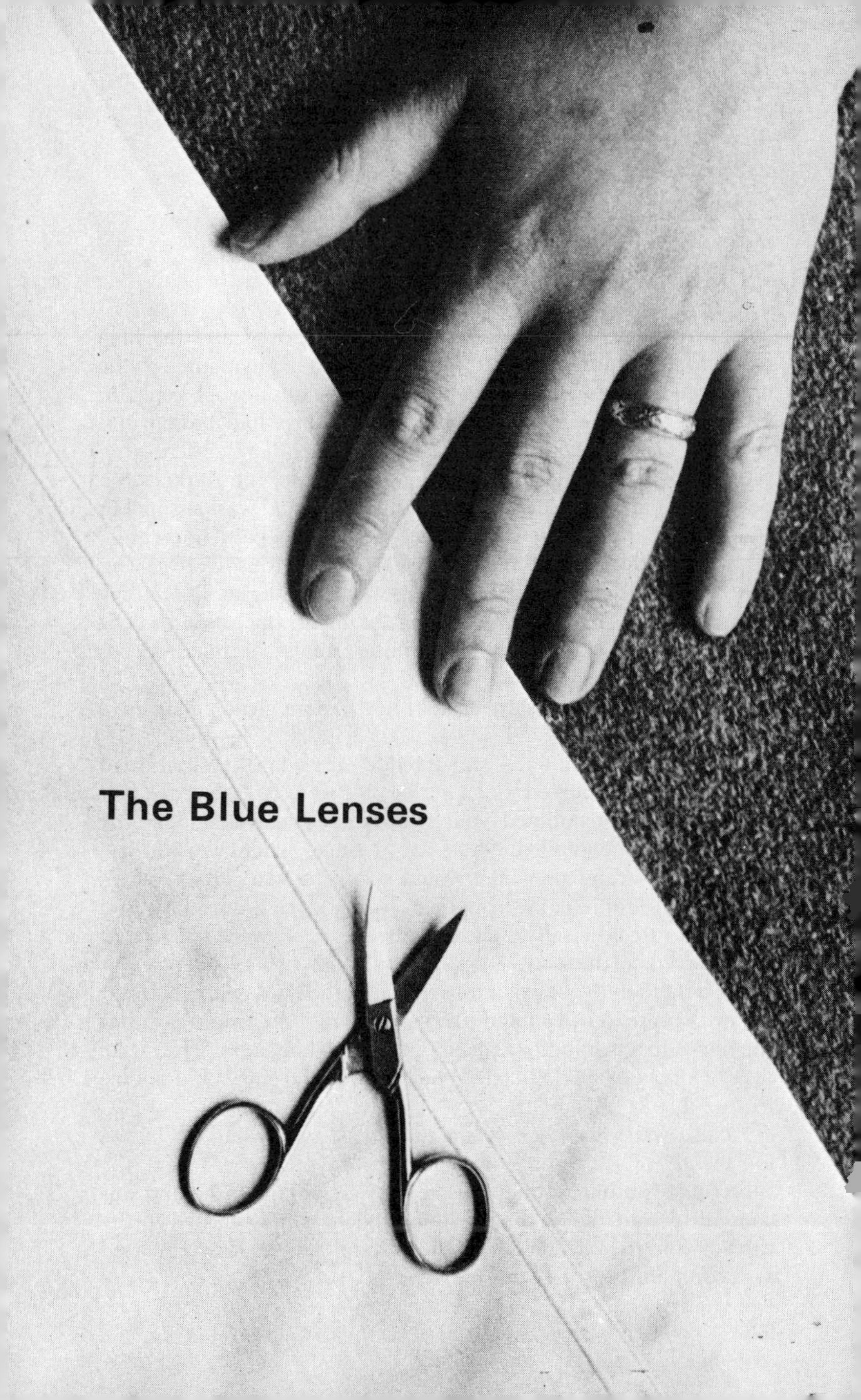

The Blue Lenses

The Blue Lenses

This was the day for the bandages to be removed and the blue lenses fitted. Marda West put her hand up to her eyes and felt the crêpe binder, and the layer upon layer of cotton-wool beneath. Patience would be rewarded at last. The days had passed into weeks since her operation, and she had lain there suffering no physical discomfort, but only the anonymity of darkness, a negative feeling that the world and the life around was passing her by. During the first few days there had been pain, mercifully allayed by drugs, and then the sharpness of this wore down, dissolved, and she was left with a sense of great fatigue, which they assured her was reaction after shock. As for the operation itself, it had been successful. Here was definite promise. A hundred per cent successful.

"You will see," the surgeon told her, "more clearly than ever before."

"But how can you tell?" she urged, desiring her slender thread of faith to be reinforced.

"Because we examined your eyes when you were under the anaesthetic," he replied, "and again since, when we put you under for a second time. We would not lie to you, Mrs West."

This reassurance came from them two or three times a day, and she had to steel herself to patience as the weeks wore by, so that she referred to the matter perhaps only once every twenty-four hours, and then by way of a trap, to catch them unawares. "Don't throw the roses out. I should like to see them," she would say, and the day-nurse would be surprised into the admission, "They'll be over before you can do that." Which meant that she would not see this week.

Actual dates were never mentioned. Nobody said, "On the fourteenth of the month you will have your eyes." And the subterfuge continued, the pretence that she did not mind and was content to wait. Even Jim, her husband, was now classed in the category of "them", the staff of the hospital, and no longer treated as a confidante.

Once, long ago, every qualm and apprehension had been admitted and shared. This was before the operation. Then, fearful of pain and blindness, she had clung to him and said, "What if I never see again, what will happen to me?" picturing herself as helpless and maimed. And Jim, whose anxiety was no less harsh than hers, would answer, "Whatever comes, we'll go through it together."

Now, for no known reason except that darkness, perhaps, had made her more sensitive, she was shy to discuss her eyes with him. The touch of his hand was the same as it had ever been, and his kiss, and the warmth of his voice; but always, during these days of waiting, she had the seed of fear that he, like the staff at the hospital, was being too kind. The kindness of those who knew towards the one who must not be told. Therefore, when at last it happened, when at his evening visit the surgeon said, "Your lenses will be fitted tomorrow," surprise was greater than joy. She could not say anything, and he had left the room before she could thank him. It was really true. The long agony had ended. She permitted herself only a last feeler, before the day-nurse went off duty – "They'll take some getting used to, and hurt a bit at first?" – her statement of fact put as a careless question. But the voice of the woman who had tended her through so many weary days replied, "You won't know you've got them, Mrs West."

Such a calm, comfortable voice, and the way she shifted the pillows and held the glass to the patient's lips, the hand smelling faintly of the Morny French Fern soap with which she washed her, these things gave confidence and implied that she could not lie.

"Tomorrow I shall see you," said Marda West, and the nurse, with the cheerful laugh that could be heard sometimes down the corridor outside, answered, "Yes, I'll give you your first shock."

It was a strange thought how memories of coming into the nursing-home were now blunted. The staff who had received her were dim shadows, the room assigned to her, where she still lay, like a wooden box built only to entrap. Even the surgeon, brisk and efficient during those two rapid consultations when he had recommended an immediate operation, was a voice rather than a presence. He gave his orders and the orders were carried out, and it was difficult to reconcile this bird-of-passage with the person who, those several weeks ago, had asked her to surrender herself to him, who had in fact worked this miracle upon the membranes and the tissues which were her living eyes.

"Aren't you feeling excited?" This was the low, soft voice of her night-nurse, who, more than the rest of them, understood what she had endured. Nurse Brand, by day, exuded a daytime brightness; she was a person of sunlight, of bearing in fresh flowers, of admitting visitors. The weather she described in the world outside appeared to be her own creation. "A real scorcher," she would say, flinging open windows, and her patient would sense the cool uniform, the starched cap, which somehow toned down the penetrating heat. Or else she might hear the steady fall of rain and feel the slight chill accompanying it. "This is going to please the gardeners, but it'll put paid to Matron's day on the river."

Meals, too, even the dullest of lunches, were made to appear delicacies through her method of introduction. "A morsel of brill *au beurre*?" she would suggest happily, whetting reluctant appetite, and the boiled fish that followed must be eaten, for all its tastelessness, because otherwise it would seem to let down Nurse Brand, who had recommended it. "Apple fritters – you can manage two, I'm sure," and the tongue began to roll the imaginary fritter, crisp as a flake and sugared, which in reality had a languid, leathery substance. And so her cheerful optimism brooked no discontent – it would be offensive to complain, lacking in backbone to admit, "Let me just lie. I don't want anything."

The night brought consolation and Nurse Ansel. She did not expect courage. At first, during pain, it had been Nurse Ansel who had administered the drugs. It was she who had smoothed the pillows and held the glass to the parched lips. Then, with the passing weeks, there had been the gentle voice and the quiet encouragement. "It will soon pass. This waiting is the worst." At night the patient had only to touch the bell, and in a moment Nurse Ansel was by the bed. "Can't sleep? I know, it's wretched for you. I'll give you just two and a half grains, and the night won't seem so long."

How compassionate, that smooth and silken voice. The imagination, making fantasies through enforced rest and idleness, pictured some reality with Nurse Ansel that was not hospital – a holiday abroad, perhaps, for the three of them, and Jim playing golf with an unspecified male companion, leaving her, Marda, to wander with Nurse Ansel. All she did was faultless. She never annoyed. The small shared intimacies of night-time brought a bond between nurse and patient that vanished with the day, and when she went off duty, at five minutes to eight in the morning, she would whisper, "Until this evening," the very whisper stimulating anticipation, as though eight o'clock that night would not be clocking-in but an assignation.

Nurse Ansel understood complaint. When Marda West said wearily, "It's been such a long day," her answering "Has it?" implied that for her too the day had dragged, that in some hostel she had tried to sleep and failed, that now only did she hope to come alive.

It was with a special secret sympathy that she would announce the evening visitor. "Here is someone you want to see, a little earlier than usual," the tone suggesting that Jim was not the husband of ten years but a troubadour, a lover, someone whose bouquet of flowers had been plucked in an enchanted garden and now brought to a balcony. "What gorgeous lilies!", the exclamation half a breath and half a sigh, so that Marda West imagined exotic dragon-petalled beauties growing to heaven, and Nurse Ansel, a little priestess, kneeling. Then, shyly, the voice would murmur, "Good evening, Mr West. Mrs West is waiting for you." She would hear the gentle closing of the door, the tip-toeing out with the lilies and the almost soundless return, the scent of the flowers filling the room.

It must have been during the fifth week that Marda West had tentatively suggested, first to Nurse Ansel and then to her husband, that perhaps when she returned home the night-nurse might go with them for the first week. It would chime with Nurse Ansel's own holiday. Just a week. Just so that Marda West could settle to home again.

"Would you like me to?" Reserve lay in the voice, yet promise too.

"I would. It's going to be so difficult at first." The patient, not knowing what she meant by difficult, saw herself as helpless still, in spite of the new lenses, and needing the protection and the reassurance that up to the present only Nurse Ansel had given her. "Jim, what about it?"

His comment was something between surprise and indulgence. Surprise that his wife considered a nurse a person in her own right, and indulgence because it was the whim of a sick woman. At least, that was how it seemed to Marda West, and later, when the evening visit was over and he had gone home, she said to the night-nurse, "I can't make out whether my husband thought it a good idea or not."

The answer was quiet yet reassuring. "Don't worry. Mr West is reconciled."

But reconciled to what? The change in routine? Three people round the table, conversation, the unusual status of a guest who, devoting herself to her hostess, must be paid? (Though the last would not be mentioned, but glossed over at the end of a week in an envelope.)

"Aren't you feeling excited?" Nurse Ansel, by the pillow, touched the bandages, and it was the warmth in the voice, the certainty that only a few hours now would bring revelation, which stifled at last all lingering doubt of success. The operation had not failed. Tomorrow she would see once more.

"In a way," said Marda West, "it's like being born again. I've forgotten how the world looks."

"Such a wonderful world," murmured Nurse Ansel, "and you've been patient for so long."

The sympathetic hand expressed condemnation of all those who had insisted upon bandages through the waiting weeks. Greater indulgence might have been granted had Nurse Ansel herself been in command and waved a wand.

"It's queer," said Marda West, "tomorrow you won't be a voice to me any more. You'll be a person."

"Aren't I a person now?"

A note of gentle teasing, of pretended reproach, which was all part of the communication between them, so soothing to the patient. This must surely, when sight came back, be forgone.

"Yes, of course, but it's bound to be different."

"I don't see why."

Even knowing she was dark and small – for so Nurse Ansel had described herself – Marda West must be prepared for surprise at the first encounter, the tilt of the head, the slant of the eyes, or perhaps some unexpected facial form like too large a mouth, too many teeth.

"Look, feel . . ." and not for the first time Nurse Ansel took her patient's hand and passed it over her own face, a little embarrassing, perhaps, because it implied surrender, the patient's hand a captive. Marda West, withdrawing it, said with a laugh, "It doesn't tell me a thing."

"Sleep, then. Tomorrow will come too soon." There came the familiar routine of the bell put within reach, the last-minute drink, the pill, and then the soft, "Good night, Mrs West. Ring if you want me."

"Thank you. Good night."

There was always a slight sense of loss, of loneliness, as the door closed and she went away, and a feeling of jealousy, too, because there were other patients who received these same mercies, and who, in pain, would also ring their bells. When she awoke – and this often happened in the small hours – Marda West would no longer picture Jim at home, lonely on his pillow, but would have an image of Nurse Ansel, seated perhaps by someone's bed, bending to give comfort, and this alone would make her reach for the bell, and press her thumb upon it, and say, when the door opened, "Were you having a nap?"

"I never sleep on duty."

She would be seated, then, in the cubby-hole midway along the passage, perhaps drinking tea or entering particulars of charts into a ledger. Or standing beside a patient, as she now stood beside Marda West.

"I can't find my handkerchief."

"Here it is. Under your pillow all the time."

A pat on the shoulder (and this in itself was a sort of delicacy), a few moments of talk to prolong companionship, and then she would be gone, to answer other bells and other requests.

"Well, we can't complain of the weather!" Now it was the day itself, and Nurse Brand coming in like the first breeze of morning, a hand on a barometer set fair. "All ready for the great event?" she asked. "We must get a move on, and keep your prettiest nightie to greet your husband."

It was her operation in reverse. This time in the same room, though, and not a stretcher, but only the deft hands of the surgeon with Nurse Brand to help him. First came the disappearance of the crêpe, the lifting of the bandages and lint, the very slight prick of an injection to dull feeling. Then he did something to her eyelids. There was no pain. Whatever he did was cold, like the slipping of ice where the bandages had been, yet soothing too.

"Now, don't be disappointed," he said. "You won't know any difference for about half an hour. Everything will seem shadowed. Then it will gradually clear. I want you to lie quietly during that time."

"I understand. I won't move."

The longed-for moment must not be too sudden. This made sense. The dark lenses, fitted inside her lids, were temporary for the first few days. Then they would be removed and others fitted.

"How much shall I see?" The question dared at last.

"Everything. But not immediately in colour. Just like wearing sunglasses on a bright day. Rather pleasant."

His cheerful laugh gave confidence, and when he and Nurse Brand had left the room she lay back again, waiting for the fog to clear and for that summer day to break in upon her vision, however subdued, however softened by the lenses.

Little by little the mist dissolved. The first object was angular, a wardrobe. Then a chair. Then, moving her head, the gradual forming of the window's shape, the vases on the sill, the flowers Jim had brought her. Sounds from the street outside merged with the shapes, and what had seemed sharp before was now in harmony. She thought to herself, "I wonder if I can cry? I wonder if the lenses will keep back tears," but, feeling the blessing of sight restored, she felt the tears as well, nothing to be ashamed of – one or two which were easily brushed away.

All was in focus now. Flowers, the wash-basin, the glass with the thermometer in it, her dressing-gown. Wonder and relief were so great that they excluded thought.

"They weren't lying to me," she thought. "It's happened. It's true."

The texture of the blanket covering her, so often felt, could now be seen as well. Colour was not important. The dim light caused by the blue lenses enhanced the charm, the softness of all she saw. It seemed to her, rejoicing in form and shape, that colour would never matter. There was time enough for colour. The blue symmetry of vision itself was all-important. To see, to feel, to blend the two together. It was indeed rebirth, the discovery of a world long lost to her.

There seemed to be no hurry now. Gazing about the small room and dwelling upon every aspect of it was richness, something to savour. Hours could be spent just looking at the room and feeling it, travelling through the window and to the windows of the houses opposite.

"Even a prisoner," she decided, "could find comfort in his cell if he had been blinded first, and had recovered his sight."

She heard Nurse Brand's voice outside, and turned her head to watch the opening door.

"Well . . . are we happy once more?"

Smiling, she saw the figure dressed in uniform come into the room, bearing a tray, her glass of milk upon it. Yet, incongruous, absurd, the head with the uniformed cap was not a woman's head at all. The thing bearing down upon her was a cow . . . a cow on a woman's body. The frilled cap was perched upon wide horns. The eyes were large and gentle, but cow's eyes, the nostrils broad and humid, and the way she stood there, breathing, was the way a cow stood placidly in pasture, taking the day as it came, content, unmoved.

"Feeling a bit strange?"

The laugh was a woman's laugh, a nurse's laugh, Nurse Brand's laugh, and she put the tray down on the cupboard beside the bed. The patient said nothing. She shut her eyes, then opened them again. The cow in the nurse's uniform was with her still.

"Confess now," said Nurse Brand, "you wouldn't know you had the lenses in, except for the colour."

It was important to gain time. The patient stretched out her hand carefully for the glass of milk. She sipped the milk slowly. The mask must be worn on purpose. Perhaps it was some kind of experiment connected with the fitting of the lenses – though how it was supposed to work she could not imagine. And it was surely taking rather a risk to spring such a surprise, and, to people weaker than herself who might have undergone the same operation, downright cruel?

"I see very plainly," she said at last. "At least, I think I do."

Nurse Brand stood watching her, with folded arms. The broad uniformed figure was much as Marda West had imagined it, but that cow's head tilted, the ridiculous frill of the cap perched on the horns . . . where did the head join the body, if mask it in fact was?

"You don't sound too sure of yourself," said Nurse Brand. "Don't say you're disappointed, after all we've done for you."

The laugh was cheerful, as usual, but she should be chewing grass, the slow jaws moving from side to side.

"I'm sure of myself," answered her patient, "but I'm not so sure of you. Is it a trick?"

"Is what a trick?"

"The way you look . . . your . . . face?"

Vision was not so dimmed by the blue lenses that she could not distinguish a change of expression. The cow's jaw distinctly dropped.

"Really, Mrs West!" This time the laugh was not so cordial. Surprise was very evident. "I'm as the good God made me. I dare say he might have made a better job of it."

The nurse, the cow, moved from the bedside towards the

window and drew the curtains more sharply back, so that the full light filled the room. There was no visible join to the mask: the head blended to the body. Marda West saw how the cow, if she stood at bay, would lower her horns.

"I didn't mean to offend you," she said, "but it *is* just a little strange. You see . . ."

She was spared explanation because the door opened and the surgeon came into the room. At least, the surgeon's voice was recognizable as he called, "Hullo! How goes it?", and his figure in the dark coat and the sponge-bag trousers was all that an eminent surgeon's should be, but . . . that terrier's head, ears pricked, the inquisitive, searching glance? In a moment surely he would yap, and a tail wag swiftly?

This time the patient laughed. The effect was ludicrous. It must be a joke. It was, it had to be; but why go to such expense and trouble, and what in the end was gained by the deception? She checked her laugh abruptly as she saw the terrier turn to the cow, the two communicate with each other soundlessly. Then the cow shrugged its too ample shoulders.

"Mrs West thinks us a bit of a joke," she said. But the nurse's voice was not over-pleased.

"I'm all for that," said the surgeon. "It would never do if she took a dislike to us, would it?"

Then he came and put his hand out to his patient, and bent close to observe her eyes. She lay very still. He wore no mask either. None, at least, that she could distinguish. The ears were pricked, the sharp nose questing. He was even marked, one ear black, the other white. She could picture him at the entrance to a fox's lair, sniffing, then quick on the scent scuffing down the tunnel, intent upon the job for which he was trained.

"Your name ought to be Jack Russell," she said aloud.

"I beg your pardon?"

He straightened himself but still stood beside the bed, and the bright eye had a penetrating quality, one ear cocked.

"I mean," Marda West searched for words, "the name seems to suit you better than your own."

She felt confused. Mr Edmund Greaves, with all the letters after him on the plate in Harley Street, what must he think of her?

"I know a James Russell," he said to her, "but he's an orthopaedic surgeon and breaks your bones. Do you feel I've done that to you?"

His voice was brisk, but he sounded a little surprised, as Nurse

Brand had done. The gratitude which was owed to their skill was not forthcoming.

"No, no, indeed," said the patient hastily, "nothing is broken at all, I'm in no pain. I see clearly. Almost too clearly, in fact."

"That's as it should be," he said, and the laugh that followed resembled a short sharp bark.

"Well, nurse," he went on, "the patient can do everything within reason except remove the lenses. You've warned her, I suppose?"

"I was about to, sir, when you came in."

Mr Greaves turned his pointed terrier nose to Marda West.

"I'll be in on Thursday," he said, "to change the lenses. In the meantime, it's just a question of washing out the eyes with a solution three times a day. They'll do it for you. Don't touch them yourself. And above all don't fiddle with the lenses. A patient did that once and lost his sight. He never recovered it."

"If you tried that," the terrier seemed to say, "you would get what you deserved. Better not make the attempt. My teeth are sharp."

"I understand," said the patient slowly. But her chance had gone. She could not now demand an explanation. Instinct warned her that he would not understand. The terrier was saying something to the cow, giving instructions. Such a sharp staccato sentence, and the foolish head nodded in answer. Surely on a hot day the flies would bother her – or would the frilled cap keep insects away?

As they moved to the door the patient made a last attempt.

"Will the permanent lenses," she asked, "be the same as these?"

"Exactly the same," yapped the surgeon, "except that they won't be tinted. You'll see the natural colour. Until Thursday, then."

He was gone, and the nurse with him. She could hear the murmur of voices outside the door. What happened now? If it was really some kind of test, did they remove their masks instantly? It seemed to Marda West of immense importance that she should find this out. The trick was not truly fair: it was a misuse of confidence. She slipped out of bed and went to the door. She could hear the surgeon say, "One and a half grains. She's a little overwrought. It's the reaction, of course."

Bravely, she flung open the door. They were standing there in the passage, wearing the masks still. They turned to look at her, and the sharp bright eyes of the terrier, the deep eyes of the cow, both held reproach, as though the patient, by confronting them, had committed a breach of etiquette.

"Do you want anything, Mrs West?" asked Nurse Brand.

Marda West stared beyond them down the corridor. The whole floor was in the deception. A maid, carrying dust-pan and brush, coming from the room next door, had a weasel's head upon her small body, and the nurse advancing from the other side was a little prancing kitten, her cap coquettish on her furry curls, the doctor beside her a proud lion. Even the porter, arriving at that moment in the lift opposite, carried a boar's head between his shoulders. He lifted out luggage, uttering a boar's heavy grunt.

The first sharp prick of fear came to Marda West. How could they have known she would open the door at that minute? How could they have arranged to walk down the corridor wearing masks, the other nurses and the other doctor, and the maid appear out of the room next door, and the porter come up in the lift? Something of her fear must have shown in her face, for Nurse Brand, the cow, took hold of her and led her back into her room.

"Are you feeling all right, Mrs West?" she asked anxiously.

Marda West climbed slowly into bed. If it was a conspiracy what was it all for? Were the other patients to be deceived as well?

"I'm rather tired," she said. "I'd like to sleep."

"That's right," said Nurse Brand, "you got a wee bit excited."

She was mixing something in the medicine glass, and this time, as Marda West took the glass, her hand trembled. Could a cow see clearly how to mix medicine? Supposing she made a mistake?

"What are you giving me?" she asked.

"A sedative," answered the cow.

Buttercups and daisies. Lush green grass. Imagination was strong enough to taste all three in the mixture. The patient shuddered. She lay down on her pillow and Nurse Brand drew the curtains close.

"Now just relax," she said, "and when you wake up you'll feel so much better." The heavy head stretched forward – in a moment it would surely open its jaws and moo.

The sedative acted swiftly. Already a drowsy sensation filled the patient's limbs.

Soon peaceful darkness came, but she awoke, not to the sanity she had hoped for, but to lunch brought in by the kitten. Nurse Brand was off duty.

"How long must it go on for?" asked Marda West. She had

resigned herself to the trick. A dreamless sleep had restored energy and some measure of confidence. If it was somehow necessary to the recovery of her eyes, or even if they did it for some unfathomable reason of their own, it was their business.

"How do you mean, Mrs West?" asked the kitten, smiling. Such a flighty little thing, with its pursed-up mouth, and even as it spoke it put a hand to its cap.

"This test on my eyes," said the patient, uncovering the boiled chicken on her plate. "I don't see the point of it. Making yourselves such guys. What is the object?"

The kitten, serious, if a kitten could be serious, continued to stare at her. "I'm sorry, Mrs West," she said, "I don't follow you. Did you tell Nurse Brand you couldn't see properly yet?"

"It's not that I can't see," replied Marda West. "I see perfectly well. The chair is a chair. The table is a table. I'm about to eat boiled chicken. But why do you look like a kitten, and a tabby kitten at that?"

Perhaps she sounded ungracious. It was hard to keep her voice steady. The nurse – Marda West remembered the voice, it was Nurse Sweeting, and the name suited her – drew back from the trolley-table.

"I'm sorry," she said, "if I don't come up to scratch. I've never been called a cat before."

Scratch was good. The claws were out already. She might purr to the lion in the corridor, but she was not going to purr to Marda West.

"I'm not making it up," said the patient. "I see what I see. You are a cat, if you like, and Nurse Brand's a cow."

This time the insult must sound deliberate. Nurse Sweeting had fine whiskers to her mouth. The whiskers bristled.

"If you please, Mrs West," she said, "will you eat your chicken, and ring the bell when you are ready for the next course?"

She stalked from the room. If she had a tail, thought Marda West, it would not be wagging, like Mr Greaves's, but twitching angrily.

No, they could not be wearing masks. The kitten's surprise and resentment had been too genuine. And the staff of the hospital could not possibly put on such an act for one patient, for Marda West alone – the expense would be too great. The fault must lie in the lenses, then. The lenses, by their very nature, by some quality beyond the layman's understanding, must transform the person who was perceived through them.

A sudden thought struck her, and pushing the trolley-table aside she climbed out of bed and went over to the dressing-table. Her own face stared back at her from the looking-glass. The dark lenses concealed the eyes, but the face was at least her own.

"Thank heaven for that," she said to herself, but it swung her back to thoughts of trickery. That her own face should seem unchanged through the lenses suggested a plot, and that her first idea of masks had been the right one. But why? What did they gain by it? Could there be a conspiracy amongst them to drive her mad? She dismissed the idea at once – it was too fanciful. This was a reputable London nursing-home, and the staff was well known. The surgeon had operated on royalty. Besides, if they wanted to send her mad, or kill her even, it would be simple enough with drugs. Or with anaesthetics. They could have given her too much anaesthetic during the operation, and just let her die. No one would take the roundabout way of dressing up staff and doctors in animals' masks.

She would try one further proof. She stood by the window, the curtain concealing her, and watched for passers-by. For the moment there was no one in the street. It was the lunch-hour, and traffic was slack. Then, at the other end of the street, a taxi crossed, too far away for her to see the driver's head. She waited. The porter came out from the nursing-home and stood on the steps, looking up and down. His boar's head was clearly visible. He did not count, though. He could be part of the plot. A van drew near, but she could not see the driver . . . yes, he slowed as he went by the nursing-home and craned from his seat, and she saw the squat frog's head, the bulging eyes.

Sick at heart, she left the window and climbed back into bed. She had no further appetite and pushed away her plate, the rest of the chicken untasted. She did not ring her bell, and after a while the door opened. It was not the kitten. It was the little maid with the weasel's head.

"Will you have plum tart or ice cream, madam?" she asked.

Marda West, her eyes half-closed, shook her head. The weasel, shyly edging forward to take the tray, said, "Cheese, then, and coffee to follow?"

The head joined the neck without any fastening. It could not be a mask, unless some designer, some genius, had invented masks that merged with the body, blending fabric to skin.

"Coffee only," said Marda West.

The weasel vanished. Another knock on the door and the kitten was back again, her back arched, her fluff flying. She plonked the coffee down without a word, and Marda West, irritated – for surely, if anyone was to show annoyance, it should be herself? – said sharply, "Shall I pour you some milk in the saucer?"

The kitten turned. "A joke's a joke, Mrs West," she said, "and I can take a laugh with anyone. But I can't stick rudeness."

"Miaow," said Marda West.

The kitten left the room. No one, not even the weasel, came to remove the coffee. The patient was in disgrace. She did not care. If the staff of the nursing-home thought they could win this battle, they were mistaken. She went to the window again. An elderly cod, leaning on two sticks, was being helped into a waiting car by the boar-headed porter. It could not be a plot. They could not know she was watching them. Marda went to the telephone and asked the exchange to put her through to her husband's office. She remembered a moment afterwards that he would still be at lunch. Nevertheless, she got the number, and as luck had it he was there.

"Jim . . . Jim, darling."

"Yes?"

The relief to hear the loved familiar voice. She lay back on the bed, the receiver to her ear.

"Darling, when can you get here?"

"Not before this evening, I'm afraid. It's one hell of a day, one thing after another. Well, how did it go? Is everything OK?"

"Not exactly."

"What do you mean? Can't you see? Greaves hasn't bungled it, has he?"

How was she to explain what had happened to her? It sounded so foolish over the telephone.

"Yes, I can see. I can see perfectly. It's just that . . . that all the nurses look like animals. And Greaves, too. He's a fox terrier. One of those little Jack Russells they put down the foxes' holes."

"What on earth are you talking about?"

He was saying something to his secretary at the same time, something about another appointment, and she knew from the tone of his voice that he was very busy, very busy, and she had chosen the worst time to ring him up. "What do you mean about Jack Russell?" he repeated.

Marda West knew it was no use. She must wait till he came. Then she would try to explain everything, and he would be able to find out for himself what lay behind it.

"Oh, never mind," she said. "I'll tell you later."

"I'm sorry," he told her, "but I really am in a tearing hurry. If the lenses don't help you, tell somebody. Tell the nurses, the Matron."

"Yes," she said, "yes."

Then she rang off. She put down the telephone. She picked up a magazine, one left behind at some time or other by Jim himself, she supposed. She was glad to find that reading did not hurt her eyes. Nor did not blue lenses make any difference, for the photographs of men and women looked normal, as they had always done. Wedding groups, social occasions, débutantes, all were as usual. It was only here, in the nursing-home itself and in the street outside, that they were different.

It was much later in the afternoon that Matron called in to have a word with her. She knew it was Matron because of her clothes. But inevitably now, without surprise, she observed the sheep's head.

"I hope you're quite comfortable, Mrs West?"

A note of gentle inquiry in the voice. A suspicion of a baa?

"Yes, thank you."

Marda West spoke guardedly. It would not do to ruffle the Matron. Even if the whole affair was some gigantic plot, it would be better not to aggravate her.

"The lenses fit well?"

"Very well."

"I'm so glad. It was a nasty operation, and you've stood the period of waiting so very well."

That's it, thought the patient. Butter me up. Part of the game, no doubt.

"Only a few days, Mr Greaves said, and then you will have them altered and the permanent ones fitted."

"Yes, so he said."

"It's rather disappointing not to observe colour, isn't it?"

"As things are, it's a relief."

The retort slipped out before she could check herself. The Matron smoothed her dress. And if you only knew, thought the patient, what you look like, with that tape under your sheep's chin, you would understand what I mean.

"Mrs West ..." The Matron seemed uncomfortable, and turned her sheep's head away from the woman in the bed. "Mrs West, I hope you won't mind what I'm going to say, but our nurses do a fine job here and we are all very proud of them. They work long hours, as you know, and it is not really very kind to mock them, although I am sure you intended it in fun."

Baa. . . . Baa. . . . Bleat away. Marda West tightened her lips.

"Is it because I called Nurse Sweeting a kitten?"

"I don't know what you called her, Mrs West, but she was quite distressed. She came to me in the office nearly crying."

Spitting, you mean. Spitting and scratching. Those capable little hands are really claws.

"It won't happen again."

She was determined not to say more. It was not her fault. She had not asked for lenses that deformed, for trickery, for make believe.

"It must come very expensive," she added, "to run a nursing-home like this."

"It is," said the Matron. Said the sheep. "It can only be done because of the excellence of the staff, and the cooperation of all our patients."

The remark was intended to strike home. Even a sheep can turn.

"Matron," said Marda West, "don't let's fence with each other. What is the object of it all?"

"The object of what, Mrs West?"

"This tomfoolery, this dressing up." There, she had said it. To enforce her argument she pointed at the Matron's cap. "Why pick on that particular disguise? It's not even funny."

There was silence. The Matron, who had made as if to sit down to continue her chat, changed her mind. She moved slowly to the door.

"We, who were trained at St Hilda's, are proud of our badge," she said. "I hope, when you leave us in a few days, Mrs West, that you will look back on us with greater tolerance than you appear to have now."

She left the room. Marda West picked up the magazine she had thrown down, but the matter was dull. She closed her eyes. She opened them again. She closed them once more. If the chair had become a mushroom and the table a haystack, then the blame could have been put on the lenses. Why was it only people had changed? What was so wrong with people? She kept her eyes shut when her tea was brought her, and when the voice said pleasantly, "Some flowers for you, Mrs West," she did not even open them, but waited for the owner of the voice to leave the room. The flowers were carnations. The card was Jim's. And the message on it said, "Cheer up. We're not as bad as we seem."

She smiled, and buried her face in the flowers. Nothing false about them. Nothing strange about the scent. Carnations were carnations, fragrant, graceful. Even the nurse on duty who came to put them in water could not irritate her with her pony's head. After all, it was a trim little pony, with a white star on its forehead. It would do well in the ring. "Thank you," smiled Marda West.

The curious day dragged on, and she waited restlessly for eight o'clock. She washed and changed her nightgown, and did her hair. She drew her own curtains and switched on the bedside lamp. A strange feeling of nervousness had come upon her. She realized, so strange had been the day, that she had not once thought about Nurse Ansel. Dear, comforting, bewitching Nurse Ansel. Nurse Ansel, who was due to come on duty at eight. Was she also in the conspiracy? If she was, then Marda West would have a showdown. Nurse Ansel would never lie. She would go up to her, and put her hands on her shoulders, and take the mask in her two hands, and say to her, "There, now take it off. You won't deceive me." But if it was the lenses, if all the time it was the lenses that were at fault, how was she to explain it?

She was sitting at the dressing-table, putting some cream on her face, and the door must have opened without her being aware; but she heard the well-known voice, the soft beguiling voice, and it said to her, "I nearly came before. I didn't dare. You would have thought me foolish." It slid slowly into view, the long snake's head, the twisting neck, the pointed barbed tongue swiftly thrusting and swiftly withdrawn, it came into view over her shoulders, through the looking-glass.

Marda West did not move. Only her hand, mechanically, continued to cream her cheek. The snake was not motionless: it turned and twisted all the time, as though examining the pots of cream, the scent, the powder.

"How does it feel to see yourself again?"

Nurse Ansel's voice emerging from the head seemed all the more grotesque and horrible, and the very fact that as she spoke the darting tongue spoke too paralysed action. Marda West felt sickness rise in her stomach, choking her, and suddenly physical reaction proved too strong. She turned away, but as she did so the steady hands of the nurse gripped her, she suffered herself to be led to her bed, she was lying down, eyes closed, the nausea passing.

"Poor dear, what have they been giving you? Was it the

sedative? I saw it on your chart," and the gentle voice, so soothing and so calm, could only belong to one who understood. The patient did not open her eyes. She did not dare. She lay there on the bed, waiting.

"It's been too much for you," said the voice. "They should have kept you quiet, the first day. Did you have visitors?"

"No."

"Nevertheless, you should have rested. You look really pale. We can't have Mr West seeing you like this. I've half a mind to telephone him to stay away."

"No . . . please, I want to see him. I must see him."

Fear made her open her eyes, but directly she did so the sickness gripped her again, for the snake's head, longer than before, was twisting out of its nurse's collar, and for the first time she saw the hooded eye, a pin's head, hidden. She put her hand over her mouth to stifle her cry.

A sound came from Nurse Ansel, expressing disquiet.

"Something has turned you very sick," she said. "It can't be the sedative. You've often had it before. What was the dinner this evening?"

"Steamed fish. I wasn't hungry."

"I wonder if it was fresh. I'll see if anyone has complained. Meanwhile, lie still, dear, and don't upset yourself."

The door quietly opened and closed again, and Marda West, disobeying instructions, slipped from her bed and seized the first weapon that came to hand, her nail-scissors. Then she returned to her bed again, her heart beating fast, the scissors concealed beneath the sheet. Revulsion had been too great. She must defend herself, should the snake approach her. Now she was certain that what was happening was real, was true. Some evil force encompassed the nursing-home and its inhabitants, the Matron, the nurses, the visiting doctors, her surgeon – they were all caught up in it, they were all partners in some gigantic crime, the purpose of which could not be understood. Here, in Upper Watling Street, the malevolent plot was in process of being hatched, and she, Marda West, was one of the pawns; in some way they were to use her as an instrument.

One thing was very certain. She must not let them know that she suspected them. She must try and behave with Nurse Ansel as she had done hitherto. One slip, and she was lost. She must pretend to be better. If she let sickness overcome her, Nurse Ansel might bend over her with that snake's head, that darting tongue.

The door opened and she was back. Marda West clenched her hands under the sheet. Then she forced a smile.

"What a nuisance I am," she said. "I felt giddy, but I'm better now."

The gliding snake held a bottle in her hand. She came over to the wash-basin and, taking the medicine-glass, poured out three drops.

"This should settle it, Mrs West," she said, and fear gripped the patient once again, for surely the words themselves constituted a threat. "This should settle it" – settle what? Settle her finish? The liquid had no colour, but that meant nothing. She took the medicine-glass handed to her, and invented a subterfuge.

"Could you find me a clean handkerchief, in the drawer there?"

"Of course."

The snake turned its head, and as it did so Marda West poured the contents of the glass on to the floor. Then fascinated, repelled, she watched the twisting head peer into the contents of the dressing-table drawer, search for a handkerchief, and bring it back again. Marda West held her breath as it drew near the bed, and this time she noticed that the neck was not the smooth glow-worm neck that it had seemed on first encounter, but had scales upon it, zig-zagged. Oddly, the nurse's cap was not ill-fitting. It did not perch incongruously as had the caps of kitten, sheep and cow. She took the handkerchief.

"You embarrass me," said the voice, "staring at me so hard. Are you trying to read my thoughts?"

Marda West did not answer. The question might be a trap.

"Tell me," the voice continued, "are you disappointed? Do I look as you expected me to look?"

Still a trap. She must be careful. "I think you do," she said slowly, "but it's difficult to tell with the cap. I can't see your hair."

Nurse Ansel laughed, the low, soft laugh that had been so alluring during the long weeks of blindness. She put up her hands, and in a moment the whole snake's head was revealed, the flat, broad top, the tell-tale adder's V. "Do you approve?" she asked.

Marda West shrank back against her pillow. Yet once again she forced herself to smile.

"Very pretty," she said, "very pretty indeed."

The cap was replaced, the long neck wriggled, and then, deceived, it took the medicine-glass from the patient's hand and put it back upon the wash-basin. It did not know everything.

"When I go home with you," said Nurse Ansel, "I needn't wear uniform – that is, if you don't want me to. You see, you'll be a private patient then, and I your personal nurse for the week I'm with you."

Marda West felt suddenly cold. In the turmoil of the day she had forgotten the plans. Nurse Ansel was to be with them for a week. It was all arranged. The vital thing was not to show fear. Nothing must seem changed. And then, when Jim arrived, she would tell him everything. If he could not see the snake's head as she did – and indeed, it was possible that he would not, if her hypervision was caused by the lenses – he must just understand that for reasons too deep to explain she no longer trusted Nurse Ansel, could not, in fact, bear her to come home. The plan must be altered. She wanted no one to look after her. She only wanted to be home again, with him.

The telephone rang on the bedside-table and Marda West seized it, as she might seize salvation. It was her husband.

"Sorry to be late," he said. "I'll jump into a taxi and be with you right away. The lawyer kept me."

"Lawyer?" she asked.

"Yes, Forbes & Millwall, you remember, about the trust fund."

She had forgotten. There had been so many financial discussions before the operation. Conflicting advice, as usual. And finally Jim had put the whole business into the hands of the Forbes & Millwall people.

"Oh, yes. Was it satisfactory?"

"I think so. Tell you directly."

He rang off, and looking up she saw the snake's head watching her. No doubt, thought Marda West, no doubt you would like to know what we were saying to one another.

"You must promise not to get too excited when Mr West comes." Nurse Ansel stood with her hand upon the door.

"I'm not excited. I just long to see him, that's all."

"You're looking very flushed."

"It's warm in here."

The twisting neck craned upward, then turned to the window. For the first time Marda West had the impression that the snake was not entirely at its ease. It sensed tension. It knew, it could not help but know, that the atmosphere had changed between nurse and patient.

"I'll open the window just a trifle at the top."

If you were all snake, thought the patient, I could push you through. Or would you coil yourself round my neck and strangle me?

The window was opened, and pausing a moment, hoping perhaps for a word of thanks, the snake hovered at the end of the bed. Then the neck settled in the collar, the tongue darted rapidly in and out, and with a gliding motion Nurse Ansel left the room.

Marda West waited for the sound of the taxi in the street outside. She wondered if she could persuade Jim to stay the night in the nursing-home. If she explained her fear, her terror, surely he would understand. She would know in an instant if he had sensed anything wrong himself. She would ring the bell, make a pretext of asking Nurse Ansel some question, and then, by the expression on his face, by the tone of his voice, she would discover whether he saw what she saw herself.

The taxi came at last. She heard it slow down, and then the door slammed and, blessedly, Jim's voice rang out in the street below. The taxi went away. He would be coming up in the lift. Her heart began to beat fast, and she watched the door. She heard his footstep outside, and then his voice again – he must be saying something to the snake. She would know at once if he had seen the head. He would come into the room either startled, not believing his eyes, or laughing, declaring it a joke, a pantomime. Why did he not hurry? Why must they linger there, talking, their voices hushed?

The door opened, the familiar umbrella and bowler hat the first objects to appear round the corner, then the comforting burly figure, but – God . . . no . . . please God, not Jim too, not Jim, forced into a mask, forced into an organization of devils, of liars . . . Jim had a vulture's head. She could not mistake it. The brooding eye, the blood-tipped beak, the flabby folds of flesh. As she lay in sick and speechless horror, he stood the umbrella in a corner and put down the bowler hat and the folded overcoat.

"I gather you're not too well," he said, turning his vulture's head and staring at her, "feeling a bit sick and out of sorts. I won't stay long. A good night's rest will put you right."

She was too numb to answer. She lay quite still as he approached the bed and bent to kiss her. The vulture's beak was sharp.

"It's reaction, Nurse Ansel says," he went on, "the sudden shock of being able to see again. It works differently with different people. She says it will be much better when we get you home."

We . . . Nurse Ansel and Jim. The plan still held, then.

"I don't know," she said faintly, "that I want Nurse Ansel to come home."

"Not want Nurse Ansel?" He sounded startled. "But it was you who suggested it. You can't suddenly chop and change."

There was no time to reply. She had not rung the bell, but Nurse Ansel herself came into the room. "Cup of coffee, Mr West?" she said. It was the evening routine. Yet tonight it sounded strange, as though it had been arranged outside the door.

"Thanks, Nurse, I'd love some. What's this nonsense about not coming home with us?" The vulture turned to the snake, the snake's head wriggled, and Marda West knew, as she watched them, the snake with darting tongue, the vulture with his head hunched between his man's shoulders, that the plan for Nurse Ansel to come home had not been her own after all; she remembered now that the first suggestion had come from Nurse Ansel herself. It had been Nurse Ansel who had said that Marda West needed care during convalescence. The suggestion had come after Jim had spent the evening laughing and joking and his wife had listened, her eyes bandaged, happy to hear him. Now, watching the smooth snake whose adder's V was hidden beneath the nurse's cap, she knew why Nurse Ansel wanted to return with her, and she knew too why Jim had not opposed it, why in fact he had accepted the plan at once, had declared it a good one.

The vulture opened its blood-stained beak. "Don't say you two have fallen out?"

"Impossible." The snake twisted its neck, looked sideways at the vulture, and added, "Mrs West is just a little bit tired tonight. She's had a trying day, haven't you, dear?"

How best to answer? Neither must know. Neither the vulture, nor the snake, nor any of the hooded beasts surrounding her and closing in, must ever guess, must ever know.

"I'm all right," she said. "A bit mixed-up. As Nurse Ansel says, I'll be better in the morning."

The two communicated in silence, sympathy between them. That, she realized now, was the most frightening thing of all. Animals, birds and reptiles had no need to speak. They moved, they looked, they knew what they were about. They would not destroy her, though. She had, for all her bewildered terror, the will to live.

"I won't bother you," said the vulture, "with these documents tonight. There's no violent hurry anyway. You can sign them at home."

"What documents?"

If she kept her eyes averted she need not see the vulture's head. The voice was Jim's, steady and reassuring.

"The trust fund papers Forbes & Millwall gave me. They suggest I should become a co-director of the fund."

The words struck a chord, a thread of memory belonging to the weeks before her operation. Something to do with her eyes. If the operation was not successful she would have difficulty in signing her name.

"What for?" she asked, her voice unsteady. "After all, it is my money."

He laughed. And, turning to the sound, she saw the beak open. It gaped like a trap, and then closed again.

"Of course it is," he said. "That's not the point. The point is that I should be able to sign for you, if you should be ill or away."

Marda West looked at the snake, and the snake, aware, shrank into its collar and slid towards the door. "Don't stay too long, Mr West," murmured Nurse Ansel. "Our patient must have a real rest tonight."

She glided from the room and Marda West was left alone with her husband. With the vulture.

"I don't propose to go away," she said, "or be ill."

"Probably not. That's neither here nor there. These fellows always want safeguards. Anyway, I won't bore you with it now."

Could it be that the voice was over-casual? That the hand, stuffing the document into the pocket of the greatcoat, was a claw? This was a possibility, a horror, perhaps, to come. The bodies changing too, hands and feet becoming wings, claws, hoofs, paws, with no touch of humanity left to the people about her. The last thing to go would be the human voice. When the human voice went, there would be no hope. The jungle would take over, multitudinous sounds and screams coming from a hundred throats.

"Did you really mean that," Jim asked, "about Nurse Ansel?"

Calmly she watched the vulture pare his nails. He carried a file in his pocket. She had never thought about it before – it was part of Jim, like his fountain pen and his pipe. Yet now there was reasoning behind it: a vulture needed sharp claws for tearing its victim.

"I don't know," she said. "It seemed to me rather silly to go home with a nurse, now that I can see again."

He did not answer at once. The head sank deeper between the shoulders. His dark city suit was like the humped feathers of a large brooding bird. "I think she's a treasure," he said. "And you're bound to feel groggy at first. I vote we stick to the plan. After all, if it doesn't work we can always send her away."

"Perhaps," said his wife.

She was trying to think if there was anyone left whom she could trust. Her family was scattered. A married brother in South Africa, friends in London, no one with whom she was intimate. Not to this extent. No one to whom she could say that her nurse had turned into a snake, her husband into a vulture. The utter hopelessness of her position was like damnation itself. This was her hell. She was quite alone, coldly conscious of the hatred and cruelty about her.

"What will you do this evening?" she asked quietly.

"Have dinner at the club, I suppose," he answered. "It's becoming rather monotonous. Only two more days of it, thank goodness. Then you'll be home again."

Yes, but once at home, once back there, with a vulture and a snake, would she not be more completely at their mercy than she was here?

"Did Greaves say Thursday for certain?" she asked.

"He told me so this morning, when he telephoned. You'll have the other lenses then, the ones that show colour."

The ones that would show the bodies too. That was the explanation. The blue lenses only showed the heads. They were the first test. Greaves, the surgeon, was in this too, very naturally. He had a high place in the conspiracy – perhaps he had been bribed. Who was it, she tried to remember, who had suggested the operation in the first place? Was it the family doctor, after a chat with Jim? Didn't they both come to her together and say that this was the only chance to save her eyes? The plot must lie deep in the past, extend right back through the months, perhaps the years. But, in heaven's name, for what purpose? She sought wildly in her memory to try to recall a look, or sign, or word which would give her some insight into this dreadful plot, this conspiracy against her person or her sanity.

"You look pretty peaky," he said suddenly. "Shall I call Nurse Ansel?"

"No . . ." It broke from her, almost a cry.

"I think I'd better go. She said not to stay long."

He got up from the chair, a heavy, hooded figure, and she closed her eyes as he came to kiss her good night. "Sleep well, my poor pet, and take it easy."

In spite of her fear she felt herself clutch at his hand.

"What is it?" he asked.

The well-remembered kiss would have restored her, but not the stab of the vulture's beak, the thrusting blood-stained beak. When he had gone she began to moan, turning her head upon the pillow.

"What am I to do?" she said. "What am I to do?"

The door opened again and she put her hand to her mouth. They must not hear her cry. They must not see her cry. She pulled herself together with a tremendous effort.

"How are you feeling, Mrs West?"

The snake stood at the bottom of the bed, and by her side the house physician. She had always liked him, a young pleasant man, and although like the others he had an animal's head it did not frighten her. It was a dog's head, an Aberdeen's, and the brown eyes seemed to quiz her. Long ago, as a child, she had owned an Aberdeen.

"Could I speak to you alone?" she asked.

"Of course. Do you mind, nurse?" He jerked his head at the door, and she had gone. Marda West sat up in bed and clasped her hands.

"You'll think me very foolish," she began, "but it's the lenses. I can't get used to them."

He came over, the trustworthy Aberdeen, head cocked in sympathy.

"I'm sorry about that," he said. "They don't hurt you, do they?"

"No," she said, "no, I can't feel them. It's just that they make everyone look strange."

"They're bound to do that, you know. They don't show colour." His voice was cheerful, friendly. "It comes as a bit of a shock when you've worn bandages so long," he said, "and you mustn't forget you were pulled about quite a bit. The nerves behind the eyes are still very tender."

"Yes," she said. His voice, even his head, gave her confidence. "Have you known people who've had this operation before?"

"Yes, scores of them. In a couple of days you'll be as right as rain." He patted her on the shoulder. Such a kindly dog. Such a sporting, cheerful dog, like the long-dead Angus. "I'll tell you another thing," he continued. "Your sight may be better after this than it's ever been before. You'll actually see more clearly in every way. One patient told me that it was as though she had been wearing spectacles all her life, and then, because of the operation, she realized she saw all her friends and her family as they really were."

"As they really were?" She repeated his words after him.

"Exactly. Her sight had always been poor, you see. She had thought her husband's hair was brown, but in reality it was red, bright red. A bit of a shock at first. But she was delighted."

The Aberdeen moved from the bed, patted the stethoscope on his jacket, and nodded his head. "Mr Greaves did a wonderful job on you, I can promise you that," he said. "He was able to strengthen a nerve he thought had perished. You've never had the use of it before – it wasn't functioning. So who knows, Mrs West, you may have made medical history. Anyway, sleep well and the best of luck. See you in the morning. Good night." He trotted from the room. She heard him call good night to Nurse Ansel as he went down the corridor.

The comforting words had turned to gall. In one sense they were a relief, because his explanation seemed to suggest there was no plot against her. Instead, like the woman patient before her with the deepened sense of colour, she had been given vision. She used the words he had used himself. Marda West could see people as they really were. And those whom she had loved and trusted most were in truth a vulture and a snake . . .

The door opened and Nurse Ansel, with the sedative, entered the room.

"Ready to settle down, Mrs West?" she asked.

"Yes, thank you."

There might be no conspiracy, but even so all trust, all faith, were over.

"Leave it with a glass of water. I'll take it later."

She watched the snake put the glass on the bedside-table. She watched her tuck in the sheet. Then the twisting neck peered closer and the hooded eyes saw the nail-scissors half-hidden beneath the pillow.

"What have you got there?"

The tongue darted and withdrew. The hand stretched out for the scissors. "You might have cut yourself. I'll put them away, shall I, for safety's sake?"

Her one weapon was pocketed, not replaced on the dressing-table. The very way Nurse Ansel slipped the scissors into her pocket suggested that she knew of Marda West's suspicions. She wanted to leave her defenceless.

"Now, remember to ring your bell if you want anything."

"I'll remember."

The voice that had once seemed tender was over-smooth and false. How deceptive are ears, thought Marda West, what traitors to truth. And for the first time she became aware of her own new latent power, the power to tell truth from falsehood, good from evil.

"Good night, Mrs West."

"Good night."

Lying awake, her bedside clock ticking, the accustomed traffic sounds coming from the street outside, Marda West decided upon her plan. She waited until eleven o'clock, an hour past the time when she knew that all the patients were settled and asleep. Then she switched out her light. This would deceive the snake, should she come to peep at her through the window-slide in the door. The snake would believe that she slept. Marda West crept out of bed. She took her clothes from the wardrobe and began to dress. She put on her coat and shoes and tied a scarf over her head. When she was ready she went to the door and softly turned the handle. All was quiet in the corridor. She stood there motionless. Then she took one step across the threshold and looked to the left, where the nurse on duty sat. The snake was there. The snake was sitting crouched over a book. The light from the ceiling shone upon her head, and there could be no mistake. There were the trim uniform, the white starched front, the stiff collar, but rising from the collar the twisting neck of the snake, the long, flat, evil head.

Marda West waited. She was prepared to wait for hours. Presently the sound she hoped for came, the bell from a patient. The snake lifted its head from the book and checked the red light on the wall. Then, slipping on her cuffs, she glided down the corridor to the patient's room. She knocked and entered. Directly she had disappeared Marda West left her own room and went to the head of the staircase. There was no sound. She listened carefully, and then crept downstairs. There were four flights, four floors, but the stairway itself was not visible from the cubby-hole where the night nurses sat on duty. Luck was with her.

Down in the main hall the lights were not so bright. She waited at the bottom of the stairway until she was certain of not being observed. She could see the night-porter's back – his head was not visible, for he was bent over his deck – but when it straightened she noticed the broad fish face. She shrugged her shoulders. She had not dared all this way to be frightened by a fish. Boldly she walked through the hall. The fish was staring at her.

"Do you want anything, madam?" he said.

He was as stupid as she expected. She shook her head.

"I'm going out. Good night," she said, and she walked straight past him, out of the swing-door, and down the steps into the street. She turned swiftly to the left, and, seeing a taxi at the further end, called and raised her hand. The taxi slowed and waited. When she came to the door she saw that the driver had the squat black face of an ape. The ape grinned. Some instinct warned her not to take the taxi.

"I'm sorry," she said. "I made a mistake."

The grin vanished from the face of the ape. "Make up your mind, lady," he shouted, and let in his clutch and swerved away.

Marda West continued walking down the street. She turned right, and left, and right again, and in the distance she saw the lights of Oxford Street. She began to hurry. The friendly traffic drew her like a magnet, the distant lights, the distant men and women. When she came to Oxford Street she paused, wondering of a sudden where she should go, whom she could ask for refuge. And it came to her once again that there was no one, no one at all; because the couple passing her now, a toad's head on a short black body clutching a panther's arm, could give her no protection, and the policeman standing at the corner was a baboon, the woman talking to him a little prinked-up pig. No one was human, no one was safe, the man a pace or two behind her was like Jim, another vulture. There were vultures on the pavement opposite. Coming towards her, laughing, was a jackal.

She turned and ran. She ran, bumping into them, jackals, hyenas, vultures, dogs. The world was theirs, there was no human left. Seeing her run they turned and looked at her, they pointed, they screamed and yapped, they gave chase, their footsteps followed her. Down Oxford Street she ran, pursued by them, the night all darkness and shadow, the light no longer with her, alone in an animal world.

"Lie quite still, Mrs West, just a small prick. I'm not going to hurt you."

She recognized the voice of Mr Greaves, the surgeon, and dimly she told herself that they had got hold of her again. She was back at the nursing-home, and it did not matter now – she might as well be there as anywhere else. At least in the nursing-home the animal heads were known.

They had replaced the bandages over her eyes, and for this she was thankful. Such blessed darkness, the evil of the night hidden.

"Now, Mrs West, I think your troubles are over. No pain and no confusion with these lenses. The world's in colour again."

The bandages were being lightened after all. Layer after layer removed. And suddenly everything was clear, was day, and the face of Mr Greaves smiled down at her. At his side was a rounded, cheerful nurse.

"Where are your masks?" asked the patient.

"We didn't need masks for this little job," said the surgeon. "We were only taking out the temporary lenses. That's better, isn't it?"

She let her eyes drift round the room. She was back again all right. This was the shape, there was the wardrobe, the dressing-table, the vases of flowers. All in natural colour, no longer veiled. But they could not fob her off with stories of a dream. The scarf she had put round her head before slipping away in the night lay on the chair.

"Something happened to me, didn't it?" she said. "I tried to get away."

The nurse glanced at the surgeon. He nodded his head.

"Yes," he said, "you did. And, frankly. I don't blame you. I blame myself. Those lenses I inserted yesterday were pressing upon a tiny nerve, and the pressure threw out your balance. That's all over now."

His smile was reassuring. And the large warm eyes of Nurse Brand – it must surely be Nurse Brand – gazed down at her in sympathy.

"It was very terrible," said the patient. "I can never explain how terrible."

"Don't try," said Mr Greaves. "I can promise you it won't happen again."

The door opened and the young physician entered. He too was smiling. "Patient fully restored?" he asked.

"I think so," said the surgeon. "What about it, Mrs West?"

Marda West stared gravely at the three of them, Mr Greaves, the house physician and Nurse Brand, and she wondered what palpitating wounded tissue could so transform three individuals into prototypes of an animal kingdom, what cell linking muscle to imagination.

"I thought you were dogs," she said. "I thought you were a hunt terrier, Mr Greaves, and that you were an Aberdeen."

The house physician touched his stethoscope and laughed.

"But I am," he said, "it's my native town. Your judgement was not wholly out, Mrs West. I congratulate you."

Marda West did not join in the laugh.

"That's all right for you," she said. "Other people were not so pleasant." She turned to Nurse Brand. "I thought you were a cow," she said, "a kind cow. But you had sharp horns."

This time it was Mr Greaves who took up the laugh. "There you are, nurse," he said, "just what I've often told you. Time they put you out to grass and to eat the daisies."

Nurse Brand took it in good part. She straightened the patient's pillows and her smile was benign. "We get called some funny things from time to time," she said. "That's all part of our job."

The doctors were moving towards the door, still laughing, and Marda West, sensing the normal atmosphere, the absence of all strain, said, "Who found me, then? What happened? Who brought me back?"

Mr Greaves glanced back at her from the door. "You didn't get very far, Mrs West, and a damn good job for you, or you mightn't be here now. The porter followed you."

"It's all finished with now," said the house physician, "and the episode lasted five minutes. You were safely in your bed before any harm was done, and I was here. So that was that. The person who really had the full shock was poor Nurse Ansel when she found you weren't in your bed."

Nurse Ansel. . . . The revulsion of the night before was not so easily forgotten. "Don't say our little starlet was an animal too?" smiled the house doctor. Marda West felt herself colour. Lies would have to begin. "No," she said quickly, "no, of course not."

"Nurse Ansel is here now," said Nurse Brand. "She was so upset when she went off duty that she wouldn't go back to the hostel to sleep. Would you care to have a word with her?"

Apprehension seized the patient. What had she said to Nurse Ansel in the panic and fever of the night? Before she could answer the house doctor opened the door and called down the passage.

"Mrs West wants to say good morning to you," he said. He was smiling all over his face. Mr Greaves waved his hand and was gone, Nurse Brand went after him, and the house doctor, saluting with his stethoscope and making a mock bow, stepped back against the wall to admit Nurse Ansel. Marda West stared, then tremulously began to smile, and held out her hand.

"I'm sorry," she said, "you must forgive me."

How could she have seen Nurse Ansel as a snake! The hazel eyes, the clear olive skin, the dark hair trim under the frilled cap. And that smile, that slow, understanding smile.

"Forgive you, Mrs West?" said Nurse Ansel. "What have I to forgive you for? You've been through a terrible ordeal."

Patient and nurse held hands. They smiled at one another. And, oh heaven, thought Marda West, the relief, the thankfulness, the load of doubt and despair that was swept away with the new-found sight and knowledge.

"I still don't understand what happened," she said, clinging to the nurse. "Mr Greaves tried to explain. Something about a nerve."

Nurse Ansel made a face towards the door. "He doesn't know himself," she whispered, "and he's not going to say either, or he'll find himself in trouble. He fixed those lenses too deep, that's all. Too near a nerve. I wonder it didn't kill you."

She looked down at her patient. She smiled with her eyes. She was so pretty, so gentle. "Don't think about it," she said. "You're going to be happy from now on. Promise me?"

"I promise," said Marda West.

The telephone rang, and Nurse Ansel let go her patient's hand and reached for the receiver. "You know who this is going to be," she said. "Your poor husband." She gave the receiver to Marda West.

"Jim . . . Jim, is that you?"

The loved voice sounding so anxious at the other end. "Are you all right?" he said. "I've been through to Matron twice, she said she would let me know. What the devil has been happening?"

Marda West smiled and handed the receiver to the nurse.

"You tell him," she said.

Nurse Ansel held the receiver to her ear. The skin of her hand was olive smooth, the nails gleaming with a soft pink polish.

"Is that you, Mr West?" she said. "Our patient gave us a fright, didn't she?" She smiled and nodded at the woman in the bed. "Well, you don't have to worry any more. Mr Greaves changed the lenses. They were pressing on a nerve, and everything is now all right. She can see perfectly. Yes, Mr Greaves said we could come home tomorrow."

The endearing voice blended to the soft colouring, the hazel eyes. Marda West reached once more for the receiver.

"Jim, I had a hideous night," she said. "I'm only just beginning to understand it now. A nerve in the brain . . ."

"So I gather," he said. "How damnable. Thank God they traced it. That fellow Greaves can't have known his job."

"It can't happen again," she said. "Now the proper lenses are in, it can't happen again."

"It had better not," he said, "or I'll sue him. How are you feeling in yourself?"

"Wonderful," she said, "bewildered, but wonderful."

"Good girl," he said. "Don't excite yourself. I'll be along later."

His voice went. Marda West gave the receiver to Nurse Ansel, who replaced it on the stand.

"Did Mr Greaves really say I could go home tomorrow?" she asked.

"Yes, if you're good." Nurse Ansel smiled and patted her patient's hand. "Are you sure you still want me to come with you?" she asked.

"Why, yes," said Marda West. "Why, it's all arranged."

She sat up in bed and the sun came streaming through the window, throwing light on the roses, the lilies, the tall-stemmed iris. The hum of traffic outside was close and friendly. She thought of her garden waiting for her at home, and her own bedroom, her own possessions, the day-by-day routine of home to be taken up again with sight restored, the anxiety and fear of the past months put away for ever.

"The most precious thing in the world," she said to Nurse Ansel, "is sight. I know now. I know what I might have lost."

Nurse Ansel, hands clasped in front of her, nodded her head in sympathy. "You've got your sight back," she said, "that's the miracle. You won't ever lose it now."

She moved to the door. "I'll slip back to the hostel and get some rest," she said. "Now I know everything is well with you I'll be able to sleep. Is there anything you want before I go?"

"Give me my face-cream and my powder," said the patient, "and the lipstick and the brush and comb."

Nurse Ansel fetched the things from the dressing-table and put them within reach upon the bed. She brought the hand-mirror, too, and the bottle of scent, and with a little smile of intimacy sniffed at the stopper. "Gorgeous," she murmured. "This is what Mr West gave you, isn't it?"

Already, thought Marda West, Nurse Ansel fitted in. She saw herself putting flowers in the small guest-room, choosing the right books, fitting a portable wireless in case Nurse Ansel should be bored in the evenings.

"I'll be with you at eight o'clock."

The familiar words, said every morning now for so many days and weeks, sounded in her ear like a melody, loved through repetition. At last they were joined to the individual, the person who smiled, the one whose eyes promised friendship and loyalty.

"See you this evening."

The door closed. Nurse Ansel had gone. The routine of the nursing-home, broken by the fever of the night before, resumed its usual pattern. Instead of darkness, light. Instead of negation, life.

Marda West took the stopper from the scent-bottle and put it behind her ears. The fragrance filtered, becoming part of the warm, bright day. She lifted the hand-mirror and looked into it. Nothing changed in the room, the street noises penetrated from outside, and presently the little maid who had seemed a weasel yesterday came in to dust the room. She said, "Good morning," but the patient did not answer. Perhaps she was tired. The maid dusted, and went her way.

Then Marda West took up the mirror and looked into it once more. No, she had not been mistaken. The eyes that stared back at her were doe's eyes, wary before sacrifice, and the timid deer's head was meek, already bowed.

Points for Discussion and Suggestions for Writing

(Suggestions for writing are marked with an asterisk.)

The Birds

1 How many different types of bird does Daphne du Maurier mention in this story? See if you can identify them with the aid of a handbook of wild birds. Notice especially the size and physical characteristics of each.

2 What impulse, according to Nat Hocken's observation, seems to affect the birds in autumn? How, as a consequence, do they behave? What are the first signs of strangeness in the birds' behaviour this particular autumn? What explanation is suggested?

3 What, after his examination of their heaped bodies in the children's bedroom the next morning, strikes Nat as peculiar about the way the birds first attacked his cottage?

4 Why is so much of what happens in this story blamed by different people on the weather? What other things in daily life do we tend to attribute to changes or unusual developments in the weather?

5 Daphne du Maurier depicts Nat's cottage as being both remote and rather primitive. By means of which details does she manage this? How is this important to the story?

6 How does Nat try to reassure his children about the birds? Why does he do so in spite of his own misgivings? Can you think of occasions from your own experience when you have done something similar in order to help reassure someone younger than yourself?

7 For what reasons does Nat go to the farm (page 8) on the Tuesday morning in spite of the fact that it is his day off?

8 Why, when he has seen the sight of the gulls at sea, does Nat hesitate to report the matter to the authorities? How would you have behaved under similar circumstances?

9 "A kind of excitement seized Nat" (page 11). Have you ever felt a thrill of excitement when confronted with the responsibility for coping with some special problem?

10 In what sense is taking precautions against the birds similar for Nat to his wartime experiences? What emergency precautions does he take at the different stages of the story? Where do his chief problems lie?

11 Why is Nat so critical of and irritated by what he imagines to be the uncaring attitude of Mr and Mrs Trigg, the radio newsreader and the telephone operator?

12 "They ought to do something" (page 13). Together with other members of your class improvise a meeting either of the Cabinet or of a town council in which methods are discussed of coping with the bird problem. Don't forget to include the difficulties as well as the advantages of certain courses of action.

13 What is odd about the behaviour of the gulls once they have risen off the sea? (page 14). What impression of careful organisation are we given by the description of their movements and those of the other birds Nat observes while he waits for the bus?

14 Why does Nat not explain to the children why they shouldn't play in the lane? Do you think it right that – at times of emergency – people (adults as well as youngsters) should be kept in the dark about things and merely ordered about by those in authority?

15 Mr Trigg scorns the idea of boarding up his windows (page 18), saying "They like to scare you on the wireless." Are there any things you can think of in life today at which people laugh or which they ignore even though they are advised to do them for their own good? Discuss both sides of the argument.

16 Why does Daphne du Maurier choose a gannet as the chief attacker when Nat is trying to get into his cottage? Look up the entry on the gannet in your birdbook.

17 Why does Nat want the wireless on? (page 20). What concerns him about what he hears?

18 How do the birds steadily adapt themselves to the problem of breaking into the cottage?

19 In what ways does Nat try to save his wife and children from realising the full horror of their situation?

20 What is the significance of the failure of the news broadcasts to come through?

21 Why does Nat not want his wife and children to go down to the farm? (page 30).

22 There seem to be advantages and disadvantages for Nat and his family in living in their remote little cottage under the circumstances. What would you say these are?

23 "Its night-time" says Johnny at just after two in the afternoon. Do you think there is an ironical significance in his childish remark?

24 What do you suppose are Nat's real feelings at the end of the story?

25 What does Daphne du Maurier intend us to imagine will happen when the story ends? Is her account of these events more effective because she leaves them in mid air?

*26 Imagine the development across the country of an emergency situation similar to that recounted in *The Birds*. Write a series of news bulletins in which the story is unfolded little by little.

*27 Study carefully the details of what Nat finds on his second visit to the Trigg farm (after the birds have attacked the place). Reconstruct and write an account of what happened during the night.

*28 "The Telephonist's Story". Tell the story of the growing emergency as sensed by the telephonist from the reports 'phoned in to her during her duty spell. Show how she might have taken the matter as a joke at first, then how she began to be bored, then how she realised the full drama of the situation. How did it affect her in the end?

*29 Write a history-book account of "The Year of the Birds" in which, from a detached point of view, you tell how the plague started and how it was eventually overcome.

*30 Write a suspense story in which – as in *The Birds* – the final result is left unstated and uncertain.

*31 Write a character-sketch of Nat as he emerges from the story.

The Lordly Ones

32 Of what difficulties are we reminded in the story of Ben concerning the bringing up of a handicapped child? What are the problems for Ben? What are those for his parents?

33 What disasters – like that of the orange on the train (page 37) – arise simply because Ben is unable to say what he wants or feels?

34 Do you sympathise with parents or teachers who are

tempted to be strict or even harsh with handicapped children?

35 In the first paragraph of the story we are told that because of his silence Ben's parents "forget to explain things to him." How does this lead to his misunderstanding about the moors and to the final tragedy?

36 "'Is he shy?' asked the woman, and the whispers began" (page 39). What are "the whispers"?

37 What is the attitude of Ben's parents to his inability to speak and the difficulties of bringing him up? How does it affect their relationship with other people (for example: the passengers on the train; the woman who helps them move into their new home; their new neighbours)?

2

38 What does Ben find so attractive about the lordly ones when he first sees them? How do his thoughts about them spring from his own experiences and background? In what way does he identify with them?

39 "He wanted . . . to flaunt his parents" (page 44). Have you ever done something you knew to be unwise or wrong simply in order to get your own back on your parents or some other member of your family?

40 "Would she be angry? Would she push him away?" (page 46). Why are these worries so important to Ben?

3

41 How, when Ben sees the leader of the lordly ones defeated, does it make him think of his own family?

42 What is actually happening – although Ben does not understand it – when the leader is defeated and replaced?

43 Why do the villagers, including Ben's father, attack the ponies, the lordly ones, at the end of the story? Why does Ben suffer such anguish when they do?

44 Could this story have ended in any other way? Does it have a moral, do you think?

*45 Retell the story of Ben's adventures either from the point of view of one of his parents or from that of the "golden mother".

*46 Write about an adventure (real or imaginary) among a group of animals.

The Pool

47 "I remember, even at school, in the middle of French" (page 52). Do you, like Deborah, have moments when, even at the most unlikely times, your mind wanders off to a place that you know well and to which you are particularly attached?

48 Deborah is a highly imaginative girl. How is this brought out in the opening section of the story? She is also very good at inventing games in order to liven up whatever she is doing. Can you find examples of some of these? Do you ever do the same sort of thing?

49 "They never know" (page 53). Is this a true observation about adults? In what ways do they "never know"? How do you account for the fact?

50 What are the principal differences between Deborah and Roger? How are they summed up when, at cricket, he tells her that she is India? (page 55).

51 What evidence is there that Deborah is a very private person?

52 "Deborah did her ritual of bowing twice. If she should forget this . . . it spelt ill-luck" (page 54). Do you or did you when you were younger have rituals such as this? What were they? Why were they important to you?

53 How are Deborah's close association with and respect for the pool and its surroundings emphasised?

54 What early hints are there of the dangers of the pool? Is it a danger to Deborah? In what way? How is this danger averted on the occasion of her first visit?

55 What is the significance of the pool to Deborah?

56 Why is "washing hands . . . tidying . . . combing hair" called a farce? (page 59).

57 "Deborah . . . wondered why laughter was so near to pain" (page 62). *Is* it? And if it is, can you say why?

*58 "The secret world". Have you ever imagined the existence of a secret world around our own into which – like Deborah – you have somehow managed to gain admittance? What was it like? How was it inhabited? Write about it and how you came to enter it.

59 In what sense can there be said to be a conflict between Deborah's body and her spirit? (page 66). How is the pool involved?

60 "Which was real? This safety of the house, or the secret world?" (page 67). Discuss.

2

61 "Deb's got out of bed the wrong side" (page 68). Make a list of the evidence there is for Roger's statement. Is there any obvious reason for her ill humour?

62 "Her own violence distressed her" (page 68). Have you ever found yourself reacting to situations in a similarly uncontrollable manner?

63 What is it that eventually tames Deborah's bad mood? Do you ever have bad moods whose reason you find it difficult to explain?

3

*64 How does the heatwave affect the different characters in the story? How do you react to heatwaves? Write an account of one that you have experienced.

65 Do you suppose Deborah's sleepiness and giddiness are due only to the heat? What other reasons might there be for a girl of her age to feel as she does? What other details underline the fact that her condition is a little abnormal?

4

66 How do the others explain Deborah's nearly fatal escapade at the pool? How might she explain it to herself?

67 Agnes reassures Deborah as she lies in bed and says that pain is usual "the first time" (page 78). How does this observation tie in with other details mentioned in the course of the story?

68 "The heaviness of knowledge lay upon her, a strange, deep sorrow" (page 78). What has Deborah lost and what has she gained through her adventures?

*69 "Growing up".

*70 Dialogue on a Hot Afternoon.

*71 Write an account of Deborah's adventures as seen either by Roger or by her grandmother.

The Old Man

72 "Did I hear you asking about the Old Man?" (page 80).

What circumstances are suggested by this opening? How does Daphne du Maurier maintain the feeling of this story being part of a conversation between two people?

73 What picture of the speaker do we receive in the course of the story from his observations, his manner of speaking and his account of his own activites?

74 Which details introduced as the story progresses suggest that there is something odd about the old man and his family? Does anything that is said make you suspect that things are not at all as they first seem?

75 For which of the characters is your sympathy chiefly aroused?

76 When you have read through the story and appreciated its point, look at the following paragraph from it once again:

> After that, winter and summer, I was always down on the beach or the rocks, and they went on living their curious, remote existence, sometimes fishing in the lake, sometimes at sea. Occasionally I'd come across them in the harbour on the estuary, taking a look at the yachts anchored there, and the shipping. I used to wonder which of them made the suggestion. Perhaps suddenly he would be lured by the thought of the bustle and life of the harbour, and all the things he had either wantonly given up or had never known, and he would say to her, "Today we are going into town." And she, happy to do whatever pleased him best, followed along.

It can clearly be read in two ways. Discuss these ways – how did you understand the paragraph when you first read the story through? – how do you understand it on second reading? Find further examples of Daphne du Maurier's presentation of material in such a fashion that it can be interpreted in two distinct ways.

77 How do you explain, in animal terms, the central events of the story – the departure of the youngsters, Boy's return and his death?

78 "They were free to be together again, and there was no longer a third to divide them" (page 89). Do human children divide their parents as Boy did his?

79 How much of a surprise was the ending of the story to you on first reading? Where there any earlier details that made

you suspect that this was not a straightforward story about a human family?

*80 Write a character-sketch of the old man either as a swan or as a human being.

*81 Draw a rough sketch map of the area described in the story (the sea, the beach, the lake, the swans' nest, the streams, the plank-bridge, the marsh, and so on) taking the information you need for building it up from the story. When you have done so, compare your map with that prepared by some other member of your class. Whose works the better? You will need to read different parts of the story very carefully in order to test whether or not your maps are as they should be.

*82 Write a story in which you try – as Daphne du Maurier does in *The Old Man* – to hold back the vital point to the very last moment.

*83 Retell the story as if you were either the old man or his missus.

*84 Imagine that the characters of this story are in fact human. How might they discuss as a family the question of the children's futures or the unexpected return of Boy? Compose a stage-dialogue on one or other of these themes.

*85 Draw a strip-cartoon of the events of this story. Include only the words of the narrator.

The Blue Lenses

86 In what ways does Marda West feel cut off from life and from other people at the beginning of this story?

87 Do you feel that it is right for doctors and hospital staff to withhold information from patients about their state of health, even for their own good?

88 How, in her blindness, does Marda West distinguish between Nurse Brand and Nurse Ansel? Whom does she prefer? Why?

*89 Marda West is worried about the week immediately after she will have left hospital. Have you ever been in hospital for a serious operation? Write about your experiences and your feelings about going home.

*90 Imagine you have temporarily lost the use of your eyes like Marda West and are laid up somewhere. How would you spend your time? Write an account of the things which might preoccupy you.

91 What is Marda West's impression of Nurse Ansel's daily life – especially during her off-duty hours? In the light of the rest of the story, do you think she is right?

92 "How much shall I see?" . . . "Everything" (page 98). How accurate is this answer, bearing in mind what happens in the ensuing pages?

93 What are Marda West's reactions when she first sees Nurse Brand?

94 Why does Nurse Brand react as she does when Mrs West asks her whether her face is a "trick"?

95 What lies behind Marda West's remark to the surgeon that she sees "almost took clearly, in fact"? (page 101).

96 What features of his manner and behaviour (other than his head) make the surgeon seem to Marda rather like a terrier?

97 How do the hospital staff interpret and react to what they see as Marda West's strange behaviour and remarks?

98 Why do the relations between the staff and their patient deteriorate so dramatically when Nurse Sweeting takes over duty?

99 "Why was it only people had changed? What was so wrong with people?" (page 107). Is it possible to deduce by this stage of the story any reason for particular people to have the animal heads that they do?

100 Why is Marda West particularly worried about the arrival of Nurse Ansel?

101 What does she fear when Nurse Ansel brings her a medicine to settle her?

102 After her husband's arrival Marda begins to suspect that something more than the mere appearance of people is not as it should be. Where do her suspicions lie?

103 Why is she now suspicious about the new financial arrangements? Can you work out the details of how they are supposed to operate?

104 In her imagination, Mrs West foresees the further transformation of the animal/people. How? What does her vision of the future suggest to her?

105 To what extent is the young house physician's (the Aberdeen's) explanation of the operation (page 117) a clue to what has happened to Marda West?

106 "How deceptive are ears . . . what traitors to truth" (page 118). Would you agree with Marda West that the sounds things and people make are often poor indicators of their

true characters?

107 What is the significance of the final paragraph of the story? To what does the "sacrifice" refer?

108 How do you account for what occurs in the story? Is it all a dream or something in Marda West's imagination or is there something more to it?

109 What – if anything – do you think is the moral of the story?

*110 Write a story about a person one of whose senses (other than sight) is either heightened or distorted.

*111 Recount the story of Marda West either in the person of Nurse Brand telling a friend when on holiday or else by means of the daily medical reports written by the surgeon and his staff about their patient.

*112 "Being Ill."

*113 "Boredom."

*114 "A Weird Dream."

*115 "Emergency!"

Further Reading

Daphne du Maurier

If you have enjoyed this book, then you may like to read more of Daphne du Maurier's short stories. The following selections are easily available:

The Birds and other stories, Penguin
The Blue Lenses and other stories, Penguin
Don't Look Now and other stories, Penguin

Among Daphne du Maurier's full-length novels, the following, all published by Gollancz, are perhaps the most accessible to teenage readers:

Jamaica Inn
Rebecca
Frenchman's Creek
My Cousin Rachel

Other Writers

If it is the other-worldly or supernatural element in the stories in this book that has most appealed to you, you may like to dip into the following recent selections of sinister short-stories:

Could it be?, edited by Michael Marland, Longman Imprint Books
Sinister and Supernatural Stories, chosen by Richard Adams, Ward Lock
Horror Stories, chosen by Bryan Newton, Ward Lock
A Roald Dahl Selection, edited by Roy Blatchford, Longman Imprint Books

Likewise, if it is the care with which Daphne du Maurier depicts the experiences of childhood and growing up that has most fascinated you, you may like to investigate:

Adams, Richard, *Stories of Adolescence*, Ward Lock
Alain-Fournier, H., *Le Grand Meaulnes*, Penguin
Barstow, Stan, *Joby*, Penguin
Colette, *Ripening Seed*. Penguin

GARNER, ALAN, *The Owl Service*, Penguin; *Red Shift*, Collins
HARTLEY, L.P., *The Go-Between*, Penguin
HUGHES, RICHARD, *A High Wind in Jamaica*, Chatto
JOYCE, JAMES, *A James Joyce Selection*, Longman Imprint Books
LEE, HARPER, *To Kill a Mockingbird*, Penguin
LEE, LAURIE, *Cider with Rosie*, Longman Imprint Books
NAUGHTON, BILL, *One Small Boy*, Longman Imprint Books
THOMAS, DYLAN, *Portrait of the Artist as a Young Dog*, Dent, Aldine Paperback
WATERHOUSE, KEITH, *Billy Liar*, Longman Heritage of Literature Series

Longman Imprint Books
General Editor Michael Marland

Titles in the series
There is a Happy Land Keith Waterhouse
Nine African Stories Doris Lessing
The Experience of Colour *edited by* Michael Marland
The Human Element and other stories Stan Barstow
The Leaping Lad and other stories Sid Chaplin
Z Cars Four television scripts
Steptoe and Son Four television scripts
Conflicting Generations Five television scripts
A Sillitoe Selection *edited by* Michael Marland
Late Night on Watling Street and other stories Bill Naughton
Black Boy Richard Wright
The Millstone Margaret Drabble
Fair Stood the Wind for France H.E. Bates
Scene Scripts Seven television plays
The Experience of Work *edited by* Michael Marland
Breaking Away *edited by* Marilyn Davies *and* Michael Marland
The Kraken Wakes John Wyndham
A Hemingway Selection *edited by* Dennis Pepper
Friends and Families *edited by* Eileen *and* Michael Marland
Ten Western Stories *edited by* C.E.J. Smith
The Good Corn and other stories H.E. Bates
The Experience of Sport *edited by* John L. Foster
Loves, Hopes, and Fears *edited by* Michael Marland
The African Queen C.S. Forester
A Casual Acquaintance and other stories Stan Barstow
Eight American Stories *edited by* D.L. James
Cider with Rosie Laurie Lee
The L-Shaped Room Lynne Reid Banks
Softly, Softly Five television scripts by Elwyn Jones
The Pressures of Life Four television plays
The Experience of Prison *edited by* David Ball
Saturday Night and Sunday Morning Alan Sillitoe
A John Wain Selection John Wain
Jack Schaefer and the American West *edited by* C.E.J. Smith
Goalkeepers are Crazy Brian Glanville
A James Joyce Selection *edited by* Richard Adams
Out of the Air Five radio plays, *edited by* Alfred Bradley
Could it be? *edited by* Michael Marland
The Minority Experience *edited by* Michael Marland *and* Sarah Ray
Scene Scripts Two Five television plays
Caribbean Stories *edited by* Michael Marland

An Isherwood Selection *edited by* Geoffrey Halson
A Thomas Hardy Selection *edited by* Geoffrey Halson
While They Fought *edited by* Michael Marland *and* Robin Willcox
The Wave and other stories Liam O'Flaherty
Irish Short Stories *edited by* Frances Crowe
The Experience of Parenthood *edited by* Chris Buckton
The Experience of Love *edited by* Michael Marland
A D.H. Lawrence Selection *edited by* Geoffrey Halson
Twelve War Stories *edited by* John L. Foster
The Birds and other stories Daphne du Maurier

Companion cassettes, with readings of some of the key stories are available for the following:
The Leaping Lad and other stories; The Human Element; A Sillitoe Selection; Late Night on Watling Street; A Casual Acquaintance; Loves, Hopes and Fears; A John Wain Selection